MOTHER MAY I

S. E. GREEN

Copyright © S. E. Green, 2021

The right of S. E. Green to be identified as the author of this work has been asserted per the Copyright, Designs and Patents Act 1976. All rights reserved. No part of this publication may be reproduced, transmitted, or stored in a retrieval system, in any form or by any means, without permission in writing from the publisher, nor be otherwise circulated in any form of binding or cover other than that in which it is published and without a similar condition being imposed on the subsequent purchaser. All characters in this publication are fictitious and any resemblance to real people, alive or dead, is purely coincidental.

1

Nora reached for the Astroglide.

She stared at her perfect complexion in her perfect bathroom in her perfect mansion. She had to do this. She had to give Merrell this one last thing.

A child.

She caressed her flawless stomach, hating the stretch marks to come. She gazed at her oft described delicious breasts, loathing what would happen to them—enlarged glands, misshapen nipples, and more stretch marks.

Nora would not breastfeed. She would lie and say she couldn't produce milk. Traditionalist Merrell would be disappointed but he would believe her. He'd pity her.

Her three-carat diamond ring glinted in the bathroom light. He'd better give her something great for this sacrifice. And she didn't mean a new Mercedes. She'd been hinting at a vacation in Italy.

She tied the silk sash on her pink see-through robe. He loved pink. She hated it.

Out in the master bedroom, her husband turned on acoustic guitar music. His sex music.

She squirted a liberal amount of lubricant on her fingers and spread it inside and out. The stupid man thought she got wet just walking toward the bed.

After replacing the plastic bottle, she turned off the light and opened the bathroom door.

Merrell lay dressed in his burgundy satin robe, propped up in the king-size bed as he read his Bible.

Bookmarking the scripture with a ribbon, he glanced up. She smiled. He smiled.

He was a handsome man. The tall and dark type with a lean physique. Women flirted with him all the time. He never flirted back. He only had eyes for her.

"My bride," he said, his gaze caressing the length of her.

"My husband," she replied, as she knew he loved.

Merrell placed the Bible on the bedside table and held out his hand. He'd already dimmed the lights, setting the mood.

She glided across the gleaming wood floor. When she reached his side of the bed, his hand slid between the sleek folds of her robe and straight up her inner thigh.

When he encountered the Astroglide he hummed his approval.

Even though her husband was a TV evangelist, Nora never prayed unless she knew the cameras were focused on her. But she prayed tonight that they'd make this stupid baby he wanted.

Then she didn't have to do this again until well after the thing was born. She'd tell him her doctor said no sex during pregnancy. Merrell would believe her.

He always believed her.

She'd give him this one, but she'd yank her uterus free before pushing out another.

2

Nora held Merrell's hand as he led the way through the front door of their Palm Beach estate. Outside a limousine waited, its engine idling with the air conditioning on.

Their driver opened the back door. Nora slid in first, followed by Merrell.

On the tan leather seat sat a lap desk with several black Sharpies and a pile of photos to be autographed.

Merrell made sure she had her herbal tea first, then poured himself a coffee.

She'd rather be drinking coffee. Or vodka.

But she sipped the tea as expected. The limousine pulled away and Merrell began autographing, scrawling his usual *May God Bless You, Pastor Hodges.*

While he worked, the car wove its way along Ocean Boulevard past multimillion-dollar homes lined with ornamental fences and greenery. Palm trees swayed in the sleepy morning summer breeze coming off the ocean.

They took the bridge over into West Palm, following 98 to Palm Beach International Airport. The limousine stopped right at their jet painted with both of their faces—his dark and handsome and hers with hot-rolled blond hair and too much makeup.

Before the driver opened the back door, Merrell leaned across and placed his hand on her three-month pregnant belly.

He asked, "How are you feeling today, my sweets?"

Nora felt fine but she lied, "A little light-headed."

"My poor wife. I'll make sure you have everything you need."

"Thank you." She smiled kindly. "You're so good to me." She did love how he doted on her.

Inside the jet, she nodded to the hairdresser and makeup artist. An assistant held open a smock that Nora slid her arms through. She sat in front of a dressing mirror while they began the hot-rolled, too-much makeup routine.

Next came her outfit for the day—a white suit with tasteful beige pumps and pearls. Merrell was dressed in a crème suit. Their stylist always complemented them.

Now finished with hair and makeup, Nora sat across from Merrell as he reviewed his sermon. She got her Kindle, selected an erotica novel, and began reading. She loved Kindles for this exact reason. No one knew what was really on her screen.

Eventually, the plane landed in New York. The aircraft exit door opened. Nora peeked out the window next to her seat. Perfect. Lots of press to catch what she had in mind.

As always, Merrell let her go first. She stepped out, waving and smiling to the cameras. She proudly looked over her shoulder at Merrell. He winked. The press loved when he winked at her.

She thought it was stupid.

Holding onto the rail, she began her descent. She even

placed her hand on her holy belly for effect. She reached the last three steps, missed one, and tumbled to the tarmac. She rolled across the dirty pavement, coming to a stop in the fetal position.

A collective gasp filled the air.

People rushed to her side.

She moaned.

When she opened her eyes, she saw Merrell's concerned face.

Perfect. This would get her what she wanted. Bedridden until this damn baby came out of her.

3

Nora laid stretched out on the hospital bed. Her husband hovered anxiously as the obstetrician completed his examination. Luckily, the fall had caused spotting.

At forty-five her husband had no gray hair, but she swore he sprouted some in the hours they'd been here.

Still dressed in his crème suit, he slipped his jacket off and laid it neatly over a nearby chair. Concern, sympathy, compassion—these were etched into the lines of his face as he gently took her hand.

A quiet knock sounded on the door. It opened, and Cooper Weber, Merrell's manager, slid inside. Where Merrell was the epitome of tall, dark, and handsome, Cooper was short, fair, and unattractive.

"Are you in pain?" her husband quietly asked.

Nora delivered a bruised smile. "Not so much." She looked at the young doctor and wove the lie. "I'm concerned. I've been light-headed of late. Of course, being thirty-five, this baby is a blessing. Our travel schedule is quite full. I'd intended on going with Merrell up until the last month."

"I wouldn't advise that," the doctor cut in, as if on cue.

In the corner, Cooper quietly observed but she knew his brain was doing furious laps.

The doctor closed the clipboard where he'd been inscribing illegible notes.

"Doctor, can you give us a minute?" Cooper asked.

After the doctor left, Cooper came to stand at the foot of her bed. He and Merrell grew up together. They were as close as brothers could be without sharing blood.

She met them both on the same night at a tent revival her mama drug her to.

She'd been seventeen then and was supposed to be smoking pot one town over with her oh-so-very-bad boyfriend. But her mama had found religion again and there they were.

Merrell saw her from the stage. It turned her on. He was older and handsome. She wanted to do bad things with him.

After the revival, Merrell sent Cooper to ask about her. Her mama had been ecstatic. Nora went to meet him, mainly to flirt. There was a certain power that came with luring a God-fearing man to the dark side.

Cooper saw right through her.

She did flirt that night. And the next. And every time she saw Merrell. But he didn't cave. He dated her for years, eight to be exact. He insisted she go to college. He paid the tuition. He bought her things. Lots of things. His ministry grew. So did his assets.

She'd been dirt poor her whole life. He had the money she wanted to live the lifestyle she deserved.

He proposed. They tied the knot.

And here they were ten married years later.

Cooper still didn't like her, and the evidence of that was all over his face as he stood at the foot of her bed.

Yes, he didn't like her but he knew her worth, and she knew the buttons to push.

She stared at Cooper. "Let me think out loud for you. We're launching a new tour this week. I'm an integral part. You've got me doing press, the hospital visits, the women's outreach...It's too much to cancel. I understand." With a long-suffering sigh, she sat up. For extra emphasis, she slid her hand—the one Merrell was holding—over to rest on her belly. "I can do this."

"No," Merrell said. "I won't risk it."

"Either way, you'll get lots of sympathy, fan mail, press," Cooper mumbled, those wheels turning.

"Cooper," Merrell admonished.

Inside, Nora smirked.

Beyond the hospital room and down the corridor, the press had gathered. She'd make a grand exit, sign a few autographs, and deliver her best, humbled smile for the cameras. Then she'd go home and do whatever she wanted for the rest of the pregnancy while Merrell toured the world, delivering sermons to the masses.

4

Thirty minutes later Nora made her grand exit, complete with a wheelchair, a blanket over her lap, and her husband pushing her. Word had spread through the hospital of their arrival. Staff and patients had wandered out into the halls to witness the moment of Merrell and Nora Hodges passing by.

A major moment.

A great silence filled the halls as people stared worshipfully.

Murmurs of *God bless* and *May the Lord be with you* followed their trail.

Nora played the heroine to the hilt, even reaching out to touch hands. There was a reason why their followers adored them.

Outside, camera crews had gathered to witness her courage.

Nora had never been better. Extraordinary even as she bared the pain of an "almost miscarriage." She let the admiration transport her. She deserved all eyes on her.

A rugged and handsome man approached. In his dark

suit, he exuded self-confidence and posed a formidable figure. His presence screamed importance. His name was Hudson Davis. He was their lawyer.

He was also her lover.

Hudson and Merrell exchanged a handshake. Then Hudson leaned down and kissed her cheek. "I was worried," he whispered.

Her insides liquefied with tenderness.

Merrell followed with a kiss to the crown of her head. The cameras ignited.

"You're flying back with her?" Hudson asked Merrell and he nodded.

"I can't stay, though," Merrell said. "We canceled today's events but I have to be back here in New York for tomorrow's schedule."

"I'm here on business for a few days, then I'll be back in South Florida. I'm happy to stop in and check on Nora." Hudson looked down at her and it took everything in her not to grin.

Instead, she reached out, and tenderly took his hand. "That would be lovely, Hudson, thank you."

"Indeed," Merrell echoed.

The driver opened the limousine door. A cluster of fans pushed forward. Merrell wheeled her closer to the limousine. He was just about to help her up when she stopped him.

"Why don't we sign a few?" she suggested.

"Are you sure?" her husband asked.

"Of course." She smiled at the fans, nodding to the bodyguards. They knew the routine.

Out came the slips of paper and pens. Phones followed. She'd touched up her makeup in the hospital and posed for a few selfies. She scrawled her name. So did Merrell.

Like in the hospital, the well-wishes came.
So brave to be pregnant and doing God's work.
God bless your child.
May the Lord grant you a healthy baby.
Pregnant. Child. Baby.

Her jaw clenched as she saw the future unfold. It would no longer be the Merrell and Nora show. Their life would revolve around this thing inside of her.

It would be the focus.

Not her.

It.

5

Palatial. That was how Nora's mama described their Palm Beach estate with dollar signs *cha-chinging* in her eyes.

She thought they bought it with room for her.

They did not.

Nora would stab her eyes out before she ever allowed that woman to share a roof with her again.

Instead, Nora moved her across the country to California. Merrell bought a condo and there her mama would stay.

If Nora never saw her again it would be too soon.

But back to the estate.

At 17,000 square feet, the home commanded 1.86 acres of oceanfront property. With six bedrooms and marble baths, a Mediterranean-style pool and spa, hardwood floors upstairs, mosaic tile downstairs, and ocean views from nearly every room, it had "French finesse with a dash of the Hamptons."

That's what a reporter said who came to do an interview when they first moved in.

All Nora cared about was that its address carried the infamous moniker, Billionaire's Row.

In the living room, a new maid scrubbed the tile floor. Nora stood drinking vodka from a juice glass, watching the maid's back vibrate with the swaying motion of polishing. Sweat darkened the light blue uniform.

Nora missed their old maid. She moved back to El Salvador. It was a pain breaking in a new one.

"Don't forget to move every potted plant and clean under them as well," Nora said. She swirled her glass and sipped.

The new maid paused in her scrubbing. Then she started back up.

"The normal response is, 'Yes ma'am'."

Again, the new maid paused in her scrubbing. "Yes, ma'am," she mumbled.

Nora's eyes narrowed. "What is your name?"

"Raina Suarez," she responded without looking at Nora.

"Look at me when I speak to you."

Raina lifted her head. She didn't quite glare but the insolence was there in her dark brown eyes.

"If you don't appreciate this job, the enormous amount of money I pay, and the free room above the garage, there are plenty of Latina girls just like you who will."

Raina's jaw flexed. "I appreciate this job and the room, Mrs. Hodges. I don't want you to find another *Latina* girl. I can do this work to your standard."

For good measure, Nora stared her down for a solid minute. She wanted to humiliate her more, but the doorbell rang.

"I'll get that." She took another sip of vodka. "You go back to scrubbing."

Nora crossed the immaculate entryway. At the foyer

table, she put her vodka down. She checked her appearance in the gold-framed mirror, smoothing blond hair behind her ears. Then she opened the front door.

Hudson Davis stood there. She didn't know how a man in a suit could be so rugged, but Hudson pulled it off.

She grinned. "You're early."

"I am."

"Raina?" Nora called. "You're done with that. Go grocery shopping. Now."

He stepped inside and closed the door. They waited in the foyer, hungrily staring at each other as Raina rushed around. Minutes later she left.

With a tantalizing smile, Nora finally backed away. She kept her eyes fixed on Hudson's.

At the stairs, she turned.

He followed.

She unbuttoned her blouse, letting it trail down her back. He slipped out of his suit jacket. She moved with practiced sensual command. At the top of the stairs, she untied her wrap skirt and let it fall. He picked it up. Next came his tie, then his shirt.

In the master bedroom, she undid his belt and slid it from the loops. She popped the button and lowered his trousers. He stepped out of them. As he took his socks off, she moved toward the king-size bed.

Dressed only in a royal blue bra and panty set, she faced him. She loved this new set. It matched her eyes.

With several yards between them, she undid her bra, excited for him to see her new swollen titties. It was the only thing about this pregnancy that she loved.

He sucked in a breath.

She turned, giving him her back, and slipped from her panties.

She never needed Astroglide with Hudson.

Nora glanced over her shoulder. His lips curved into a charming grin. God, she loved that grin.

She crawled onto the bed and Hudson came toward her. He spread her legs wide and pleasured her with his mouth first. Then he plunged inside of her and she screamed as loud as she wanted.

She liked it raunchy and hard, and Hudson gave it to her over and over again.

There was nothing quiet, proper, and missionary style about sex with Hudson.

6

Months rolled by. Nora's belly grew.

December arrived and so did the annual Christmas children's event that Merrell always hosted in their home. As usual, the Christian Television Network and local media covered it.

"You'll love being surrounded by the kids," Merrell said, rubbing her ninth month stomach. "Plus, I know how cooped up you've been."

She hadn't been. Between laying out by the pool, devouring trashy magazines, weekly massages, lunchtime vodka, nighttime cigarette, and routine mani-pedis, pregnant homebound life suited her. It was amazing how many people came to you when you had the money to make it happen.

The terrace had been decorated for Christmas with wreaths, a giant tree, and piles of presents. Hired actors dressed as elves and Santa interacted with the poor children. A five-piece ensemble played cheery holiday music.

Nora sat on a lounge chair holding a two-year-old boy

on her lap. Cameras flashed as she radiated a smile and helped the child open a sparkly blue package. Merrell circulated the crowd of kids, leaning down to chat, tweak their noses, and help them with opening their gifts.

Cooper hovered in the background, doing his manager job, and making sure cameras were getting the right shots.

The lady who ran the Children's Home stood just behind Nora. She leaned down to whisper, "Words cannot express how grateful we are for this."

Nora's eyes grew moist. "I look forward to this every year."

The little boy in her lap settled his head to rest against her breast. A camera zoomed in to capture the moment. He looked up at Nora. Automatically, she smiled down into his face but then paused when her eyes met his.

Something stirred in her that she hadn't been expecting. An intensity. A longing. A tug. Her heart experienced an unfamiliar emotion.

In the distance, the ocean sparkled in the afternoon sun. Palm trees swayed in the seventy-degree breeze. A lone sailboat drifted across the horizon.

Nora's red linen dress shifted as the boy snuggled in.

She pressed her cheek to the top of his head with genuine affection. A sense of peace washed over her. She had everything in the world, but a baby.

Maybe she'd been wrong. Maybe this was what had been missing in her life. A baby was what she needed to be happy and fulfilled.

Nora had grown up wanting everything and having nothing. This baby would have a father and a mother. She could give it the world. She could show her mama how a real mother should be.

A real mother should lavish her child. She should sacrifice for her child. She should stay married and not move from man to man, looking for someone to support her.

A real mother should never leave her child locked in a closet.

7

Elizabeth Hodges was born on Christmas Day.

Smiling, Nora held her as Merrell looked on in awe.

"Look at her hands," Nora whispered, reverently touching a little fist. "They're so tiny."

"With ten perfect fingers and toes," Merrell said. He kissed Nora first, then Elizabeth.

A nurse came into their private hospital suite. She paused when she saw the family. She spoke to Elizabeth, "What a wonderful and charming life you will live."

Merrell handed the nurse his phone. "Will you take a picture?"

Nora's smile faltered. She looked down at her hospital gown and quickly calculated she hadn't washed her face in nearly twenty hours. Don't even get her started on her hair.

She looked around for a mirror.

Merrell watched her with amusement. "You look radiant. I want to remember this moment forever. Our first family photo."

Nora wanted to refuse, but she couldn't. Not in front of

the nurse. So, she played the moment to the hilt. She tilted Elizabeth toward the camera like she was the Holy Grail.

"How beautiful she is," the nurse murmured.

Nora forgot her vanity as she glanced once again down at her daughter.

The photo taken showed Merrell smiling, Elizabeth sleeping, and Nora weeping.

In the years to come, she would look back on that photo, not with fondness, but with her mama's words in her head. She'd said them the day Nora called with the pregnancy news.

You're going to hate that kid. Just wait.

WILDLY OVER-DECORATED. There was nothing tasteful about Elizabeth's nursery. If Pottery Barn Kids made it, Merrell bought it.

Nora sat in the white wingback rocking chair with her daughter cradled in her arms. Merrell stood propped in the doorway admiring the sweet moment.

"You're so beautiful," Nora cooed. "I'm going to give you everything. You'll have the life I didn't. You're a very lucky little girl."

Merrell shifted from the door and Nora glanced up with a content smile. He crossed the herringbone rug, stopping beside her. He reached for Elizabeth and Nora hugged her tight. Almost too tight.

Merrell sighed, but he backed away.

Nora began to hum as she rocked Elizabeth.

Mama's wrong. I'll never hate you. You're mine. All mine.

8

On Elizabeth's fifth birthday, they turned their home and terrace into a magical wonderland complete with a mini carousel, a chocolate fountain, pony rides on the beach, fairy-tale characters, candy sculptures, live music, and a birthday cake taller than Elizabeth.

Merrell had wanted to combine the annual Christmas children's event with Elizabeth's birthday, but Nora refused. Her daughter needed to have a day that was all hers, separate from the holiday.

So, the annual Christmas event occurred a few days earlier and today, Christmas itself, was all about her daughter's birthday.

Nora swore she'd never be one of those moms who wore matching outfits with her daughter. But there they were in identical pink dresses.

Pink, her daughter's favorite color. Just like Merrell.

Elizabeth's friends laughed and played. Adults smiled. The hired photographer took pictures.

"Smile!" the photographer said.

Nora and Elizabeth put their faces together in a practiced move, cheek-to-cheek with big grins.

"Love it!" the photographer cheered.

Nora squeezed Elizabeth. "Are you having a fabulous time?"

"Yes, Mommy! So much fun!" She spun away to join her friends.

The photographer moved away as well to capture the other events. Nora stepped lightly over to where Merrell and Cooper stood talking. Merrell opened his arm and smiling, she walked into it.

As the two men conversed, Nora's eyes tracked over the celebration. Her mama sat in a corner, drinking coffee laced with whiskey. Nora didn't invite her. She showed up unannounced this morning, leaving Nora with no choice but to let her in.

Her mama sure as heck would be gone by tomorrow. Nora would make sure of it.

She kept scanning the crowd. She spotted Elizabeth about to dip her finger into the chocolate fountain.

The photographer circled. Nora plastered a radiant smile, calling out, "Elizabeth, sweetheart, don't put your finger in the fountain!"

Her daughter heard her, glancing over with a mischievous grin. Quickly she dipped her finger in and just as quickly licked the chocolate off. The photographer scrambled to capture the moment.

Nora's smile faltered. Elizabeth had never disobeyed her before. Not even during the "terrible twos."

Giggling, Elizabeth raced from the fountain straight toward her parents. She flung herself into her daddy's arms. He laughed and kissed her cheek. Nora wasn't sure if he'd seen the defiant act or not.

Once again, the photographer circled, this time zeroing in on father and daughter. Nora repositioned herself to be in the shots. Elizabeth pressed her cheek to her daddy's and together they grinned for the camera.

That was a practiced move only mother and daughter did. How long had she been doing it with her father?

"How about some of the family down by the beach?" Cooper suggested.

Nora smiled. "I think that sounds—"

"Oh no!" Elizabeth cried. "I got chocolate on my pretty dress!"

Nora looked at the spot on her daughter's chest. *That's what happens when you don't listen to me*, she wanted to say, but instead replied, "It's fine."

"No!" Elizabeth wriggled to get down from her father. "I need it cleaned. *Please.*"

Nora looked down into her face and it struck her then how much Elizabeth looked like Merrell. Of course, Nora had noted it before but always dismissed it. At this moment, though, it mattered. Why couldn't her daughter have looked like her with blond hair and blue eyes? Why did she have to favor Merrell's dark features?

"It's fine," he said, waving their maid over. "Raina, help Elizabeth clean that spot, please."

Elizabeth looked up at Nora with an angelic victory.

Her jaw clenched.

Raina hurried over and took Elizabeth.

The birthday party continued. By the time Raina returned with Elizabeth, Nora's mood had transitioned back to a pleasant one. The family followed the photographer down to the beach.

Merrell and Nora swung Elizabeth between them, and

the camera clicked. Merrell picked Elizabeth up, and the camera clicked. She giggled, and the camera clicked. Her dark hair blew in front of her face, and the camera clicked. Merrell sat her down, and the camera clicked.

Nora kept smiling, changing her angles as their publicist had taught her.

"Doing great!" the photographer cheered.

He crouched down on Elizabeth's level. *Click. Click. Click.* He laughed. "You're quite the ham, aren't you?"

Nora stopped posing. Her smile slid away. She looked down to see Elizabeth blowing the camera a kiss.

Merrell laughed. Elizabeth took his hand and they skipped off down the beach. The enthusiastic photographer followed. Nora didn't. She stood in her bare feet watching them get further and further away.

No one noticed that Nora didn't follow.

"I told you that you'd hate her," Mama said from behind her.

That night Nora and Elizabeth sat on the terrace as the cleaning staff buzzed around. Merrell had gone down to the beach for a run.

Nora's mama had retired to one of the guest rooms. First thing tomorrow morning, Nora had a cab reserved to take her to the airport and back to California.

I told you that you'd hate her.

Nora had maintained her party smile throughout the rest of her daughter's fifth birthday, but her mama's words had played on repeat in her head. As they did now while Nora watched Elizabeth sift through her birthday gifts.

"Daddy said I get to pick two to keep. The rest we have to donate to charity."

"That's right," Nora replied, forcing yet another smile. "Which two have you decided on?"

Elizabeth picked up the personalized doll that Nora had custom ordered. She smiled at her mommy as she set it aside. "This one first," she said.

Nora's strained smile transitioned into a real one. "And the second one?"

Elizabeth picked up the Crayola Light-Up Tracing Pad that her daddy gave her. "This one."

"Good choices," Nora praised. "What are you going to name the dolly?"

"Well, Elizabeth, of course. Elizabeth the second!"

Nora laughed.

Hudson Davis came through the terrace doors, as handsome and rugged as ever. He'd been noticeably absent from the birthday party.

Their affair had stopped after Elizabeth was born. Something changed in Nora when she held her daughter that first time. She wanted to be the best mom ever. She wanted to be the good and wholesome person everyone thought she was. So, she ended the affair, but Hudson remained their lawyer and friend.

"Sorry I'm late," he said. "I was on back-to-back calls with another client."

"Uncle Hudson!" Elizabeth squealed. She jumped up and ran over to hug him.

From his suit pocket, he slid out a small white box. "I understand there's a birthday girl in the house?"

Elizabeth took the present and quickly unwrapped it. Inside rested a sterling silver necklace with a pink butterfly pendant.

"I love it!" She hopped in place, handing it back. "Will you put it on me?"

Kneeling down to her level, Hudson worked the clasp free and while she held her hair out of the way, he fastened it around her neck.

Nora watched, trying to remember the last time Hudson had given *her* a gift. She couldn't remember the occasion, but she remembered the gift—a pen etched with her initials.

A stupid pen.

Even though she hated the color pink, she'd rather have that butterfly necklace.

Nora's smile once again became forced. "Elizabeth, *sweetheart*, remember the two-present rule."

"Two-present rule?" Hudson stood.

"I get to keep two and the rest we're donating," Elizabeth said brightly.

Hudson tapped her nose. "I think that's a fabulous idea. Which two are you keeping?"

Clasping the necklace, Elizabeth turned toward Nora. "Unless...Mommy, may I keep three?"

Nora studied her daughter's pleading face. She could relent. Merrell wouldn't care.

She wasn't sure if it was the defiant chocolate fountain scene, or how she stole the photographer's heart, or the lavish attention, or the chocolate stain on Elizabeth's dress, or Mama's words, or that stupid butterfly necklace...but Nora found herself saying, "No, make a choice."

Elizabeth's face fell.

She shuffled over to where she'd placed the custom ordered doll and the Crayola Pad. She picked each item up. She studied them—back and forth and back again.

Nora held her breath, waiting to see.

Her daughter took the doll, walked it over to the pile of presents to be donated, and placed it right on top.

Elizabeth turned and looked right at Nora, and for the first time, she saw herself in her daughter. She may look like Merrell, but Elizabeth's insides were all Nora.

Defiant. Rotten. Manipulative.

9

On a Friday morning in April, Nora lounged on the terrace looking out over the beach where Elizabeth was building a sandcastle. Five days ago she went into anaphylactic shock during Merrell's Sunday broadcast. They had no idea what Elizabeth was allergic to—because that's what the doctor said had likely happened, an allergic reaction. But nine-one-one had been called, and she was rushed to the emergency room. Tests had been done and results would be in soon.

Nora wouldn't be surprised if Elizabeth had faked the whole thing. Not like she wasn't the center of attention before, but this had really put her there.

Hudson sat beside Nora. It was the first time they'd been alone since Elizabeth was born. One phone call, though, and here he was.

Merrell had left for a Christian retreat in Italy where he would be delivering the keynote address. Nora was supposed to go with him. Now she couldn't because of Elizabeth.

"How would it look?" he'd said. "She went into anaphylactic shock on national TV just a few days ago. Until we get the test results back, the two of you have to stay home."

Nora had tried not to whine when she replied, "Raina can watch her. We trust Raina. You know how much I've wanted to see Italy."

Merrell had simply stared at her.

So, here Nora sat babysitting Elizabeth while her husband toured Italy.

Once upon a time, Merrell gave Nora everything she wanted. She excelled at manipulating him. But when it came to his beloved Elizabeth, Nora never came out ahead.

Worse, she didn't know what to do. None of her old tricks worked anymore.

At least Hudson was here...

"Couldn't ask for a better spring day," Hudson said. "Clear sky, warm breeze, gorgeous water, low humidity for a change."

"Mm," Nora agreed.

With a sigh, she caressed her hands along the white crocheted maxi dress she'd just bought. She crossed her legs in a practiced move, and the slit fell open to reveal tan and lean muscles.

Hudson glanced over, as she knew he would. "You make it hard to keep my hands off of you when you wear things like that."

"Maybe I don't want you to keep your hands off of me anymore." She cut him a look.

Behind his designer sunglasses, his eyes flared with interest. He glanced down to the beach where Elizabeth played, and Nora visualized his wheels turning.

She shifted forward on the lounge chair, calling down to Elizabeth. "Go wade in the water, Elizabeth!"

Her daughter glanced up. "But I don't want to. I want to finish my sandcastle."

Nora's gaze darkened.

Elizabeth scowled.

"She's five," Hudson said. "Are you sure she can go in the water by herself?"

"She's fine. She knows not to go in beyond her knees without an adult." Nora pointed to the water. "Go wade. I'll join you in a few minutes."

Elizabeth's face brightened with that promise. "You too, Uncle Hudson?"

"I can't." He gestured to his suit. "I have to go back to work. But you have fun." He waved her on.

She got up and skipped from the castle down to the water's edge. Nora didn't waste a second. She retrieved a blanket from the terrace and draped it over both of their laps.

He'd already taken off his jacket and loosened his tie. She worked the belt free on his trousers and slid his zipper down. Her hand found its way inside his boxers and she clasped his erection. She didn't have to ask him to return the favor. He knew what to do. His hand slid up her inner thigh and he groaned when he discovered she wore no panties.

It had been over five years since they fooled around and they both reached climax quickly.

Afterward, he used the blanket to clean up. He pressed a kiss to her cheek and whispered in her ear, "I have to go but let me know when you want me to come over again."

With a content smile, Nora watched him leave. She remembered Elizabeth and glanced down to the water. But her daughter wasn't in the water. She stood beside her sandcastle staring up at Nora with a puzzled face that said it all. She'd seen what they'd done.

Nora lunged from the lounge chair, took the terrace steps down to the sand, and charged the few yards over to where her daughter was now hesitantly backing away.

Nora kicked the sandcastle.

"Mommy, no!"

She kicked it again.

"M-Mommy," her voice broke. "Don't."

She kicked it again.

Elizabeth cried. "I worked forever on that! You're being mean."

"You spoiled rotten brat." Nora grabbed Elizabeth's arm and drug her across the beach. "I told you to wade in the water. And if I tell you to do something, you do it."

"Mommy, you're hurting me." Elizabeth tugged on her arm.

Nora tightened her grip. "Good. It's about time someone disciplined you correctly."

"Mommy!" she sobbed.

Nora plunged into the water. She flung her daughter into an oncoming wave. It crashed over her head and Elizabeth flailed. She surfaced, crying and gasping for air.

Nora turned away, leaving her there, and stomped back up the beach. She kicked the rest of the sandcastle until nothing was left.

Elizabeth's sobs filled the air.

But Nora didn't care. She continued up the steps, across the terrace, and into the house. "Raina, go get Elizabeth!"

THAT NIGHT a soft knock came on Nora's bedroom door. "Mommy, may I come in?"

Nora flipped a page of the magazine she was reading. "If you must."

Elizabeth opened the door and slipped inside. Nora glanced up, watching her daughter hesitantly cross over to where she sat in the corner chaise.

Elizabeth looked down to her bare feet, nibbling her bottom lip.

She looked like Merrell when she did that. "What do you want?"

"I'm sorry I disobeyed you." Elizabeth glanced up. "I promise to be better."

Nora stared at her daughter for a long moment. Something shifted inside of her and she recognized it as remorse. Maybe she had overreacted.

She put the magazine down and took Elizabeth's little hand. "I accept your apology."

Her daughter's face curved into a relieved smile. They looked at each other and Nora sensed there was something else. Perhaps Elizabeth wanted to apologize for another incident.

"What is it?" Nora encouraged.

Quietly, her daughter asked, "What were you and Uncle Hudson doing under the blanket?"

Nora's face heated. She released Elizabeth's hand. "Nothing. My dress accidentally came undone and your uncle was helping me put it back together."

She nodded to the door, not giving Elizabeth a chance to respond. "Now leave Mommy alone before I change my mind and decide not to accept your apology."

10

Two years ticked by and their lives settled into a routine.

Sundays, Merrell delivered a televised sermon from their home church in West Palm.

Mondays through Thursdays, he traveled all over the states and beyond where he gave speeches, attended conferences, went to business meetings, and visited various charities.

Fridays, he came back from travel and worked from home.

Saturdays, he spent with Nora and Elizabeth.

Other than the book tour he went on last month and the revival tour scheduled for next month, their weeks always looked the same.

Nora loved to travel. She loved to be on stage. She used to do all of those things with him, but other than appearing during his Sunday televised sermon, Nora stayed at home.

Because of Elizabeth and her peanut allergy.

No, that wasn't fair. Really, it was because of Cooper and his polls. He was always surveying their followers and ever since her allergic episode on TV two years ago, their supporters felt Nora should be a stay-at-home mom.

And here she was.

Nora toasted the air with her glass. Fine then, at least she had vodka.

11

Early morning light filtered through the blinds and Nora struggled to sit up. Outside, seagulls cawed and she wanted to yell at them to shut up.

Merrell would be home the day after tomorrow. He'd gone to Duke to give the commencement speech.

Her empty vodka glass remained on the bedside table. On the nights that she drank she made it a habit to down what her mama called the "ultimate hangover cure": a vitamin B_{12}, coconut water, and two Advil.

Unfortunately the "ultimate hangover cure" didn't work near as well as it used to.

With a groan, she slowly made her way into the master bathroom. She flicked on the light and winced.

God, she looked horrible.

Leaning forward, she studied her puffy face. She pressed her fingers along her hairline and stretched the skin back. At forty-two, she was too young for a facelift. She'd make an appointment for Botox.

She tilted her chin and studied her neck. Her gaze narrowed in on a crease that hadn't been there yesterday. It didn't matter how many vodkas she had, Nora always remembered to moisturize at night.

She needed a new lotion. Maybe she'd try olive oil. It worked for Cleopatra.

Under the sink, she'd installed a mini-fridge and she opened it to retrieve a gelled mask. After washing her face in cold water, she strapped the chilled pack over her cheeks and eyes. She slipped out of her blue bamboo pajamas and stepped on the scale.

Three pounds heavier than yesterday.

She wouldn't drink tonight, she promised herself.

Nora switched on the extra bathroom light, making it even brighter. Without mercy, she scrutinized her naked body. She turned from side to side and grabbed a mirror for the rear view.

She'd always been naturally lean but the older she got, the more it became evident that wouldn't hold.

Especially since she had Elizabeth.

Nora swore she had another dimple in her butt. How was that even possible?

With a heavy sigh, she threw the face mask onto the counter and quickly changed into running clothes. One last glance in the mirror and she repeated what she did every morning, "You've still got it, you gorgeous bitch."

Though it was only six, she still coated her face and neck with SPF. She pulled her blond ponytail through a baseball cap and trotted downstairs.

Raina was already up and busy in the kitchen. She spied Nora and they exchanged a small nod of greeting.

Out the glass doors, across the terrace, and down to the beach she went. She opted not to warm up and went straight into a run. She had a lot of vodkas to sweat out.

With sunglasses on, she ran the sand that bordered

Billionaire's Row. A few other early risers had come down to work out as well. But there was no acknowledging one another, as everyone respected privacy here.

The sun rose. The ocean lapped to shore. Humidity clung in the still air.

The temperature climbed to ninety, and five miles later Nora worked up a proper cleanse.

She left her running shoes on the terrace, took her socks off, and wiped the sand from her feet. Drenched in sweat, she walked into the air conditioning and shivered.

In the kitchen, Raina had her morning green juice waiting.

Nora eagerly sipped it. "After my shower, I want peanut butter on sweet potato."

With a nod, Raina got a stool and retrieved the peanut butter from the highest cabinet. Peanuts—the one thing Nora loved just had to be the thing Elizabeth was allergic to.

When Merrell insisted they remove it from their kitchen, Nora had put her foot down. She loved peanut butter and ate it nearly every day. She didn't see why Elizabeth's allergy had to ruin the one thing she indulged in. She'd already given up so much for the daughter Merrell insisted they have. She held her ground, suggesting an out-of-reach cabinet.

Merrell reluctantly agreed. "But if the tiniest of anything happens, it's gone," he'd said.

"Fine," Nora had replied, rolling her eyes.

That had been two years ago now and nothing had happened.

The house phone rang then, and Raina answered. "Pastor Hodge's residence. May I help you?"

Nora sipped her juice.

"It's Mr. Weber," Raina said, handing her the phone.

"Cooper?" Nora frowned. "What's going on?"

"Merrell's not doing well."

"It's just a cold. He's had one for the past week."

"I know and it's getting worse. He's scheduled to give the commencement speech at Duke."

"I know. Tomorrow, right?"

"Right." Cooper took a breath. "I spoke to the president of the university. I suggested he find another person to deliver the commencement, and he requested you."

It took Nora a moment to comprehend what Cooper just said. She looked at Raina and grinned.

"Nora, you still there?"

"Yes! Yes, I'll do it!" She laughed.

"Okay, Merrell and I are coming home on the private jet. We'll get him settled with his doctor and then you and I will head back to Duke. The speech is already written, but we'll work on personalizing it for you."

"Yes, yes. Sounds wonderful. I'll be ready." Nora hung up. She laughed and spun a circle, suddenly feeling twenty years younger.

She grabbed Raina and danced around the kitchen. "Oh, Raina. This is what I wanted. I needed this. I'm going to do such a good job. Cooper will see. Merrell's run down. He can start staying here more, and I'll take over some of his schedule. I'll travel and see the world. This is the way it was supposed to be all along. I wasn't supposed to be here with Elizabeth. I was supposed to be out there eating the best foods. Staying in the best hotels. Talking to the press. Delivering speeches. I'm so good in front of people. I'm a natural." She let go of Raina. "Oh, and of course spreading God's word."

"Of course," Raina awkwardly agreed.

Nora whirled away. "I've got so much to do. I'll be upstairs."

She felt light as she took the arching stairwell up to the master suite. She skipped through the door, across the room, and came to a stop at the bathroom entry.

Elizabeth stood in front of the mirror, dressed in Nora's discarded pajamas. Her daughter wore the gelled face mask strapped over her head. She turned side-to-side, looking at her body. She leaned in, staring at her face. She pressed her fingers into her hairline and stretched her skin back. "You've still got it, you gorgeous bitch."

Nora's triumph fell away. She surged into the bathroom, coming up behind Elizabeth.

Her daughter gasped and spun around.

"What are you doing?" Nora demanded.

"N-nothing. I was just playing."

"Who were you imitating?"

Elizabeth didn't respond.

"Answer me!" Nora snapped.

"You, Mommy," she whispered.

Nora spun her daughter around. "Your father has spoiled you beyond repair." She grabbed the back of Elizabeth's neck and ripped the mask off.

"Mommy!" Elizabeth cried. "I was just playing."

"That's not how you play." Nora turned on the hot water and grabbed a bar of soap.

Elizabeth struggled against the grip Nora had on her neck. "I'm sorry. I'm sorry. I'm sorry."

She glared at her daughter in the mirror as she worked the soap under the heated water. Her nails dug through Elizabeth's hair, piercing the skin on the back of her neck. Her daughter's wide brown eyes filled with tears as Nora shoved her head over the sink.

"Open your mouth!"

With a whimper, Elizabeth did, and Nora scrubbed her gums and teeth with the bar.

"You will *not* use language like that in this house. You will *not* disrespect me." Nora scrubbed harder. Her daughter cried. "You will *not* touch my things without asking." She took the soap from Elizabeth's mouth. "Are we clear?"

Sobbing, her daughter spat bloody suds and chunks of soap into the sink.

"Are we clear?" Nora repeated.

"Yes," Elizabeth cried. "Yes, Mommy. I promise. I'm sorry."

"And stop calling me 'Mommy.' You're seven now. I'm your Mother." Nora threw the bar into the sink and walked from the bathroom.

To think she'd just been in a good mood.

12

The Duke commencement went far better than Nora expected. The crowd came to their feet with applause as she finished her speech.

She took her place on the stage alongside the university's president to distribute diplomas and shake hands.

Now, in the limo back to the hotel, Cooper sat across from her as she grinned and stared out the window. Hopefully, Merrell would stay sick for a while and she'd take on the rest of his May and June schedule.

Her phone rang and when Merrell's name lit up the screen, her grin spread wider.

She put him on video. "Hi!" she chirped. "It went so well. Oh, Merrell, I wish you could've seen me."

His brow twitched and he forced a tiny smile. "I'm glad."

She waited for him to say more, but he didn't.

He simply studied her.

Nora's grin slowly faded. She knew that face. He wanted to say something and didn't know how to. Instead, he lifted a tissue and coughed into it.

That cough didn't sound good.

"What'd the doctor say?" Nora asked.

"Not sure yet. They ran tests. That's not why I'm calling."

"Okay, why are you calling?"

Merrell sighed long and deep. "Have you seen Elizabeth's mouth?"

Silence.

She weighed her response. "Yes. I can't believe she did that to herself."

More silence, this time on Merrell's end.

He cleared his throat. "What do you mean?"

"I walked in our bathroom and saw her scrubbing her teeth with a bar of soap." Nora shook her head. "When I asked her what she was doing, she said she was washing her mouth out because she'd said a bad word."

Silence again.

"It didn't seem so bad when I looked at it." Nora frowned. "Why, how bad is it?"

"Her gums are rubbed raw and bleeding."

"Oh, dear..." Nora grimaced. "Bad enough for a doctor?"

Merrell didn't answer that question and instead, asked one of his own. "Didn't you tell me your mother used to do that to you when you were a child?"

Silence, this time back on Nora's end.

"What are you suggesting?" she asked, her voice even.

"Elizabeth said you did that to her."

Nora remembered Cooper was in the limo and switched the call off video. She put the phone to her ear. "Is Elizabeth there? Let me talk to her."

"I'm not sure that's a good—"

"Let. Me. Talk. To. My. Daughter."

Back to silence.

Then, "Hang on."

A moment later, Elizabeth's voice came on the line. "Hi," she said, her voice small.

"Why would you tell your father I did that to you?" Nora asked. "Do you know how serious of an accusation that is?"

"But you did do it," she quietly responded.

Nora took a breath. "You're not in trouble. But you need to tell your dad the truth. Tell him that you did that to yourself. Because if you continue with this lie, then you really will be in trouble. Do you understand me?"

Her daughter hesitated.

"Elizabeth, answer me please."

"Yes, Momm—" She stopped. "Yes, I understand."

"Good. Now keep me on the phone. I want to hear you tell your dad the truth." Nora held her breath, listening to Elizabeth speak to Merrell.

Her husband came back on the line. "I don't know what to say."

"Me either. But she's not in trouble for lying," Nora said. "She was scared. I'm not mad at her. Make sure she knows that."

"I will. I'll talk to her about the appropriate ways to deal with bad words in the future. I'll also have Raina take her to the doctor." He coughed again. "I'm happy to hear the speech went well. I'm proud of you, Nora."

Another smile creased her face, but it wasn't near the grin she'd had before the call.

They hung up and Nora looked across the limo to Cooper.

He stared back.

"What?" Her brow went up.

Cooper didn't respond. He simply keyed in his unlock code and began checking messages on his phone.

Nora went back to looking out the window.

Aside from her mama, Cooper was the only person in this world Nora couldn't fool.

13

Days later, Merrell was diagnosed. Leave it to him to be a non-smoker and come down with lung cancer.

Cooper met with them both and decisions were made.

Nora would take over Merrell's travel schedule. Ferris Palmer, the junior pastor at their home church, would take over Sunday's broadcast. And Merrell would heal.

Nora wanted and could've done it all, but she knew when to press. If she had to pick between travel or Sunday's broadcast, she would pick travel any day.

May transitioned to the summer months, summer to fall, fall to winter. The annual children's Christmas event rolled around. It was the first time in over a decade that they didn't host it. Merrell didn't want to scare the children with his sickly appearance.

Elizabeth turned eight.

Nora was the happiest she had been in a very long time.

14

Nora glided across the stage in all her royalty, reaching down to lay her hand on various heads. Behind her, the fifty-person chorus sang the last hymn of the night. Throughout the arena, prayers filled the air.

She touched another head. "I pray the Lord bless you and keep you safe."

Minutes later, her team ushered her through the back hallways. One of the tech crew timidly asked for a selfie and she obliged.

In the limo, she used hand sanitizer. "I really wish you'd screen who comes down to the stage. Some of their heads are so greasy."

Cooper ignored her as he dialed Merrell. He called her husband more than she did.

Raina answered, and he put it on speaker.

"How's our guy?" Cooper asked.

"Not so good," Raina replied. "He's sleeping. Chemo did a number on him today."

"And Elizabeth?"

"She's okay," Raina said. "She's been sleeping with him every night. It seems to help them both."

Cooper looked over at Nora, and she quickly said, "Give them both my love."

"Will do."

"Thank you, Raina," Cooper said. "We couldn't do any of this without you."

"I love them both very much. I'm happy to." Raina didn't say she loved Nora.

They hung up, and Nora stared out the limo at the Chicago skyline, majestic even in February's bitter cold. She loved Chicago. And New York. And L.A. Really any big city.

Her attention switched from the darkness outside to her reflection. She hated hot rolled and teased hair. She hated pink lipstick. "I'm so tired of this look."

Cooper didn't miss a beat. "Focus groups say it's what your followers want. You change your look, you lose popularity."

She hated his surveys and polls and focus groups. But she knew their importance. Frankly, she was just happy their supporters picked God's work over Nora being home with her sick husband.

"I know," she sighed.

Eventually, the limo pulled up outside the hotel.

In the lobby, Nora hesitated, glancing over at the bar. She wasn't ready to go to her room yet.

Cooper stopped beside her. "Not the bar."

The lobby was alive with movement. Several guests noticed her arrival and stopped to watch.

"You know how revved up I am after an event," she whispered. "It's only eleven. I can't go to my room yet."

He steered her toward the perfectly acceptable lounge. "Then let's sit here and have dessert and decaf."

She'd rather have vodka and a cigarette, but she'd take what she could get.

He helped her out of her white wool coat. They sat in the corner opposite of each other in low leather chairs with a round table between them. They ordered cheesecake and decaf. Several hotel guests hesitantly approached and she turned on the smile. She shook hands, graciously signed autographs, and posed for more selfies.

"You're so dear to me," she repeated. "Thank you."

When that died down, she settled back, sipping her coffee and glancing around the immaculate lobby. She kept a pleasant smile fixed to her face, always ready for rogue photographs. Like the woman over at the counter with her phone in the air.

People came and went. The adjacent bar livened. A blues singer crooned. A fireplace flickered.

The elevator dinged and out stepped a tall dark-haired woman followed by a handsome dark-haired man. Holding hands, she smiled over her shoulder at him. He lifted their joined fingers to kiss the back of hers.

Nora watched through the front windows as he saw her outside. They shared a long kiss before he helped her into an Uber. The car drove away and the man turned back to the hotel. He stepped into the lobby, still with that content smile. He glanced over to the bar, then scanned the lounge.

When his eyes met Nora's, his smile fell away.

"I didn't know Hudson was here," Cooper said.

15

Up in her hotel suite, Nora paced, growing angrier with each step.

Hudson lounged in an elegant corner chaise with his jacket off and his tie loose. He sipped his whiskey, watching her with amusement.

"What do you see in a woman like that? She looks nothing like me. I mean, my God, her hair is as short as yours!"

"I'm no expert. But it's called a pixie cut and it's beautiful." Another sip of whiskey.

Nora stopped pacing. She turned on him. "What does *that* mean?" She yanked at her teased and sprayed hair. "You think I enjoy looking like this?"

"No," he carefully replied. "I don't think you like looking like that."

"Why didn't you tell me you were going to be here?" she snapped.

"I didn't realize I was supposed to copy you on my schedule." He swirled the liquid in his glass.

Her jaw tightened.

"What exactly are you mad about?" he asked. "My presence or my chosen company?"

"What's her name?" Nora demanded.

Another sip. "Ah, and there it is."

"There. What. Is?"

"Last time I checked, I'm single. I can do whoever, whenever, in whatever way I want."

Her nostrils flared. "That didn't look like a hookup. That looked like…more."

"Maybe it *is* more."

She screamed.

He placed his tumbler on a side table.

"Are you picking her over me?"

Hudson didn't respond.

Her fingers curled into two fists. "You're ruining everything. I thought we had something."

"We're fuck buddies. What else did you think we were?"

Nora flinched.

"And *I'm* ruining everything?" He leaned forward. "You should rethink those words. You have everything you've always wanted. If something is 'ruined,' it's because you're doing the ruining."

Nora didn't have a response.

Hudson gentled his tone. "When I first met you I saw this beautiful, intelligent young woman who knew what she wanted. You had set your focus on success and I respected that. I understood it. But you will destroy yourself if you don't get that focus back. Your decisions aren't as smart as they used to be. You've let emotion trickle in. Where is the levelheaded girl I first met?"

Her eyes narrowed. "You're nothing but a deceitful whore. How many client wives do you sleep with? Is that who that woman was? I should tell Merrell to fire you."

Hudson was out of the chaise and across the room before Nora blinked. He grabbed her shoulders and shook her hard. "Are you insane?"

Nora crumbled against him.

"Huh?" He shook her again. "What is wrong with you?"

"I don't know," she cried. "I'm a horrible person. I know I am."

Hudson released her and Nora melted to the floor in a sobbing mess. He retrieved his jacket and walked past her toward the door.

She reached out. "Wait."

"Oh get up," he snapped. "You look ridiculous down there."

"Where are you going?" she begged.

"I'm leaving. I've had enough of your drama."

Nora quieted her voice. "Merrell will be dead soon. What if we got married?"

He turned back, an unreadable look on his face.

She stretched out on the carpeted floor, arching her spine in a sensual welcome. "Hudson," she purred. "Please."

Shaking his head, he turned the knob. "This is over. Tell Merrell to fire me. I don't care."

Then he left, ignoring Nora's scream that followed him out.

16

The following evening Nora was back in Palm Beach. She paced the guest room where Merrell now stayed. With all the chemo side effects, she couldn't sleep in the same bed.

"Now that I've taken on your responsibilities, I need my rest," she'd said.

Merrell's oxygen tank had clicked as he breathed in. "I'll have Raina move me into a guest room."

That had been months ago and a great decision. Nora did sleep so much better without him.

Now, though, she continued to pace. "I want Hudson fired."

"Why?" Merrell rasped.

She hated that rasp. She hated the oxygen tank. She hated his smell, his bald head, his sallow cheeks. Everything about him creeped her out.

Honestly, how could a person who had never smoked a day in his life be dying of lung cancer? The whole thing was ridiculous.

Nora stopped pacing. She gripped the footboard of his

bed, making herself look at him. She fixed a concerned, frightened expression on her face.

"He...tried something." She pressed her lips together. "Last night in Chicago, he came to my suite. He propositioned me, said he'd always had a thing for me. When I told him to get out, he grabbed my shoulders and shook me. Hard." Nora worked up a good set of tears. "I was so scared."

Her husband breathed in. He breathed out. The tank clicked. "I'll have it taken care of."

Nora dabbed at her eyes with the heel of her hand. She sniffed. "Thank you." She squeezed his foot tucked under the blanket. "Do you need anything?"

"Just my phone."

She retrieved it from the bedside table, handed it to him, and then pressed a kiss to his forehead as she held her breath.

At his door, she paused. "Open or closed?"

"Closed."

"I love you," she said.

"Me too," he replied.

She closed his door and nearly skipped down the hall to the stairwell. She floated down the steps, her mood lifting with each movement. She found Elizabeth and Raina in the kitchen making sugar cookies.

Even though Nora hated sugar cookies—they were Merrell's favorite—she came up behind Elizabeth and hugged her.

Her daughter stiffened.

She pressed a loud kiss to Elizabeth's cheek. "Can Mommy join in the fun?"

Her daughter shot a look at Raina, who quickly replied, "Yes, Mrs. Hodges, of course."

Nora tied an apron on as she whirled over to the iPod

docking station. She cued up *Curious George*'s soundtrack and the theme song launched.

> When everyday (everyday!) is so glorious (glorious!)
> Then everything (everything!) is so wondrous (wondrous!)

Nora recited the lyrics, dancing beside Elizabeth, occasionally bumping their hips together. She joined in making cookies, singing along, continuing to dance.

It was as the soundtrack transitioned into the next song that she realized Elizabeth wasn't dancing and singing, too.

She barely looked at Nora and instead flicked nervous glances across the island to Raina.

"What's wrong?" Nora stopped dancing. "I thought you liked *Curious George*."

Her daughter didn't answer.

Nora kept her focus on Elizabeth as she kept her focus on Raina. "Why are you looking at, Raina?" Nora took a step back, surveying Elizabeth's stiff body. "What's wrong? You look like you're scared of something."

Raina cleared her throat. "It's just that *Curious George* is more what she listened to years ago. She's older now."

"Oh." Nora kept looking at the side of Elizabeth's face. "Is that right?"

She nodded.

Nora went over to the docking station and turned the music off. She stared at the black screen, remembering a similar time. She'd been around Elizabeth's age, eight or so. Her mama was in a good mood. They danced around the kitchen, singing.

It's one of the best memories Nora had of her mama.

"Well, what do you listen to now?" she asked.

"Daddy and I have been listening to John Denver," Elizabeth quietly replied.

Nora hated John Denver. "Fine." She found a playlist and tapped it open.

As Denver's mellow voice filled the kitchen, Nora went back over to the island. This time she stood beside Raina.

They worked in silence making the sugar cookies, listening to "Sunshine on My Shoulders" transition into "You Fill Up My Senses."

The latter was the first song Merrell and Nora slow danced to.

"Listen to the lyrics," he'd whispered. "This is how I feel about you."

Nora had smiled when what she wanted to do was roll her eyes. Romance was overrated. Yet years later she'd slow danced with Hudson to that same song. She'd found herself saying that same line to Hudson that Merrell had said to her. And she'd meant it.

It wasn't often Nora displayed raw emotion.

Hudson had responded with a smile.

Now, the memory made her teeth grind.

She marched over to the docking station, and with a flour-coated finger, she jabbed John Denver off.

Silence filled the kitchen.

Nora spoke, "Dancing and singing with my mama is one of my best memories." She turned and looked at Elizabeth, surprised to discover tears had filled her own eyes. "It hurts my feelings that you'd rather listen to John Denver than sing and dance with me to *Curious George*." She untied the apron and placed it on the counter next to the docking station. "Who cares if you've outgrown *Curious George*?"

The tears tipped out to roll down Nora's cheeks. Not

knowing how to respond, Elizabeth once again glanced at Raina.

"Yeah, you hurt my feelings, Elizabeth." Nora walked from the kitchen. "One day you'll look back on this moment and wish you would have handled it differently."

17

Merrell Joshua Hodges lost his battle with lung cancer on Saturday evening in his Palm Beach, Florida estate surrounded by family and close friends. He was an American pastor, televangelist, and New York Times *best-selling author. Based in West Palm, Hodges's televised sermons were seen by approximately 10 million viewers in the US and several million more in over 100 countries weekly. He is survived by his wife, Nora Hodges, and their eight-year-old daughter, Elizabeth.*

Nora kept reading the latest posting of her husband's death. As expected, it had hit every media outlet from the US to Europe, Asia to Africa, South America to Australia, and back.

He died almost to the date, one year after his diagnosis.

She'd received condolences from presidents, dignitaries, royalty, leaders, and film, TV, and music stars.

You would've thought Princess Di had passed away again with the elaborate funeral procession, performances, and guest speakers.

Nora sat through it all, brave with the appropriate tear

here and there. Thankfully, the casket had been closed. The last thing she wanted to view was Merrell's frail and thin body. She'd seen enough of that in his last remaining weeks.

"Mrs. Hodges, I loved your husband."

"I do hope you'll reach out to us when you're feeling up to it."

"He will be missed."

"Merrell loved you so much."

Nora listened to it all, receiving hugs, all the while keeping her arm around Elizabeth, who, thankfully, maintained a courageous face throughout.

Now, Nora sat dressed in proper mourning black in Merrell's home office with Cooper beside her and Hudson across from them.

Hudson.

She couldn't believe it when he walked in carrying Merrell's will.

But she kept her jaw tightly closed and waited for the reading. As soon as she took over Hodges Ministry, firing Hudson would be the first thing she did.

She glanced at Cooper and he offered a comforting smile that came across heartfelt. Despite the friction that had always been between them, she appreciated it. She felt sure Merrell left something for Cooper.

Hudson flipped through the pages, apparently looking for the part that pertained to personal things. Nora stared at the thick Last Will and Testament. Tension and anticipation filled the air.

Cooper shifted. "Raina said she was taking Elizabeth to her sister's home for the night?"

"Yes." Nora kept staring at Hudson and the will.

"That was nice of her."

Nora nodded.

Mother May I

"Here we are," Hudson said.

Nora sat forward.

He began to read paragraphs of legal jargon that Nora ignored. She waited for the meat of things.

"I, Merrell Joshua Hodges, who resides in the city of Palm Beach..."

Nora took a breath. Here they go.

"Item one. The name of my spouse is Nora Hodges, hereinafter referred to as 'spouse.' I have one living child, Elizabeth Hodges, hereinafter referred to as 'child.'"

Nora resisted the urge to wave him on.

"Item two. I name Cooper Weber as executor of this will. I direct that all of my debts, funeral expenses, costs, and administration be paid at my executor's discretion."

Her brow furrowed. She'd researched "executor" and read that he or she managed the unfinished affairs, like closing accounts and paying debts. The executor also maintained assets and belongings. Naturally, Nora thought she'd be executor but she supposed it made sense for Cooper to do it. Merrell probably thought she'd be too distraught over his passing to manage things.

"Item three. Real property. Unless otherwise transferred by law, I give and devise to my child all of my interest in any real property and real estate maintained by me."

Nora frowned, listening closely.

"I bequeath all my tangible personal property and accounts to my child. Upon my child's death, the remaining assets will revert to the ministry per the executor's discretion."

Nora could barely move.

"The remainder of my estate, be it real, tangible, mixed...shall be donated to a charity of my executor's discretion." Hudson paused, taking a sip of water. "Item four. Distribution to my spouse."

Nora's eyes narrowed.

"For reasons known to her, I bequeath a sum of five thousand dollars per month. Should she remarry or die, this sum will revert to my child."

Nora's fingers dug into the arms of her chair.

"Item five. Guardianship. Should my spouse pass and it becomes necessary that a guardian be named for my child I appoint my executor as such."

Nora had heard the saying "seeing red" but she'd never encountered it until this moment.

"Item six. Should Cooper Weber no longer be able to manage my estate, I direct Hudson Davis as a co-executor. To the extent permitted by law, the administration of my estate..."

Nora sat in Merrell's home office, listening to Hudson read the rest. She schooled her expression. She would not give them the satisfaction of her ire.

When Hudson finished, he reorganized the papers. She didn't look at Cooper, but she suspected he knew about this. How could he not? He was Merrell's best friend and manager.

She kept her voice level. "Let me get this right. Everything Merrell owns goes to Elizabeth. Should she pass, it goes back into the ministry. I get a five thousand per month allowance as long as I don't remarry, which by the way, is half as much as I get now. The two of you control the empire. What you say goes. I do maintain guardianship of my daughter unless I die. Then even that goes to Cooper. Sound about right?"

"That is correct," Hudson said.

Nora stood up. She smoothed her palms down her black

dress, didn't look at either one of them, and with her head high, she walked from the office.

She went up to the master suite, poured herself a tumbler full of vodka, and lit a cigarette. She stood at the window that overlooked the driveway and waited for the two men to leave.

When they did, she picked up the phone and dialed the last person she expected to want right now.

Her mama.

18

Nora paced the stairs—up, down, up, down. With each pass, she glared at the framed photos lining the walls.

There were some of her and Merrell. Others of her and Elizabeth. Some with all three. Several with just Elizabeth and Merrell. And the one took the day Elizabeth was born.

Happy.

Happy.

Happy.

She tossed back the last bit of vodka and set the tumbler down on the bottom step. The alcohol flowed through her veins and up to her head with a pleasant fuzz. With as much as she'd drank since the reading of the will, she should have passed out by now. She contributed her alertness to the anger she'd yet to let go.

It needed out.

That's what her mama had said during their call. *You get good and angry about this. You fight back. No court's gonna let him get away with what he's done.*

Unfortunately, Nora wouldn't be fighting back in court.

As much as she loathed Hudson, he was the best of the best. That Last Will and Testament couldn't be broken.

But there were other things she could do.

She took the first frame off the wall and flung it through the air. She was on the bottom step and it didn't have far to go, but it landed on the tile floor with a satisfying crack.

Nora stepped up, grabbing the next couple of frames. These she tossed over her shoulder and they too made a satisfying crack.

Next step up, she slid another framed photo off its nail. She let it go overhand as if she was shooting a basket. It hit the foyer floor and shattered.

She smiled. That was more like it.

Another couple of steps and more photos. These she wound up and threw like she was pitching a baseball. The frames sailed across the foyer and smacked into the opposing wall. Glass flew in every direction.

Her smile transitioned to a snarl.

More steps, more photos. She bowled underhand, allowing them to skip down the steps. They plunked and splintered where they wanted to.

A few more steps and a few more photos until she reached the last one. The one that was taken by the nurse on the day Elizabeth was born.

"You look radiant," Merrell said. *"I want to remember this moment forever. Our first family photo."*

Nora saw that photo every time she ascended the stairs. It showed Merrell smiling, Elizabeth sleeping, and Nora weeping.

Her mama's words circled her brain.

You're going to hate that kid. Just wait.

Yeah, well, she hated Merrell more.

She took the frame, flipped it over, and worked the

picture free. She tore it into chunks and tossed them over the banister.

The pieces floated in the air.

Nora watched as they eventually fell to join the heap of glass shards, fractured frames, and other destroyed photos.

Raina would be back in the morning. She could clean all this mess up.

Satisfied, Nora glided into the master suite. She passed on more vodka and went straight for the good stuff.

A giant doobie.

She smoked the whole thing and finally passed out.

~

Late the next morning, she got out of bed and though she had a hell of a hangover, she managed a shower.

With sunglasses on, she shuffled into the kitchen. "Raina, I need coffee, eggs, bacon, buttered toast..." Her voice trailed off as she took in the scene.

A garbage can sat next to the door, filled with glass. A pile of broken frames lined the island where Raina busied herself gluing them back together. Damaged photos scattered the kitchen table where Elizabeth was taping the jagged seams.

It all came back to Nora in a satiating flash. She wanted to laugh, but instead, she frowned. "Oh my goodness. I'm so sorry. I was so terribly sad last night after Cooper and Hudson left. I couldn't bear to see Merrell's handsome face. I lost it. I was crying uncontrollably. Then I was angry." She worked up tears. "Angry that he left me and Elizabeth. I meant to get up early and clean it all, but I was so emotionally drained from the events of the past few days." She stepped toward Raina. "We can buy new frames."

"I know, but some are handmade. You can't get duplicates."

"Then let me help."

"It's okay, Mrs. Hodges. I have it. Why don't you go out to the terrace for fresh air? I'll bring your food."

"If you insist." Nora scooted over to where Elizabeth sat. She stood beside the kitchen table watching her daughter carefully tape Merrell's face back together.

For several seconds she watched the meticulous work and she began to regret what she had done. He was Elizabeth's father after all. Nora reached down, just to touch one, and Elizabeth's arms shot out to cover the photographs.

"No, let me," she said. "I want to."

Nora's fingers curled in. She didn't know what to say. She really just wanted to touch one and show her regret. She waited for a beat or two, then reached out again.

"Mother, please." Elizabeth looked up at her through her father's eyes. "Please?"

Nora withdrew her hands and folded her arms across her middle. Elizabeth's tense body relaxed. She took a piece of clear tape and carefully resumed. Nora watched her work, alternating between looking at the photos and studying her daughter's dark hair and face.

Something around her neck caught Nora's attention. "You're still wearing that butterfly pendant that Hudson gave you when you were five?"

"Sometimes," Elizabeth said. "I like it."

"Well, Uncle Hudson isn't a very nice man. You should think about that the next time you put it on." Nora walked away, making a mental note about that necklace.

19

Nora googled 'What is the proper mourning time for a spouse?'

The results varied, one site even saying a year. There was no way she'd walk around like a depressed widow for twelve whole months.

She wanted to get back to work. She'd fulfilled all of Merrell's pre-booked travel events. Ferris Palmer, the junior pastor, had taken over his weekly broadcast. She'd watched nearly every one of them, and she grudgingly admitted that he was good.

Not as good as her though.

She wasn't sure what Cooper or the board of Hodge's Ministry had in mind. Whatever it was, she deserved compensation. She'd worked years without anything official. Granted, she'd always had her monthly allowance, but things were different now. She deserved more for all of her hard work.

She wanted a spot on the board.

She gave herself ninety days to act the widow role.

She went to church every Sunday with Elizabeth. They

sat in their usual spot where the cameras could see her. She attended the women's Bible study every Wednesday.

In public, she maintained a brave face, quietly accepting condolences.

In private, she plotted the next steps. And she stewed.

For Merrell to create that will, he must have known or suspected all the lies. He saw through her. That or Cooper got to him. He'd never liked Nora, and somehow he convinced Merrell to see things his way.

When, though, did that change?

How long had it been going on?

Nora thought back through the years and all the times she manipulated Merrell to her side. Did he know all along that she was a fraud? Was he manipulating her right back?

She wanted to be angry but felt more admiration. Merrell hadn't been the milquetoast she'd thought. He could have been playing her from day one.

The sneaky bastard.

But Hudson was a different story. Merrell would have never kept Hudson on the payroll if he knew they'd slept together. However, if Cooper knew, he'd keep that secret from Merrell.

If Cooper knew...

Maybe Hudson went to Cooper and confessed their affair. The two men talked and decided on how to handle things.

Nora had an ugly side. She wasn't so narcissistic that she couldn't recognize and admit that. Very few people saw that side of her, though—her mama, Raina, Elizabeth, and Cooper and Hudson.

She bet the two men were having a big laugh about all of this.

Yet, Cooper knew her worth. Hodges Ministry wouldn't

be the multibillion dollar empire without Merrell *and* Nora. She'd more than proven that during Merrell's absence.

She should call Cooper's bluff. If she threatened to leave, she'd wager her measly five-thousand monthly allowance that he'd cough up more to keep her.

Yes, she'd make Cooper think she was falling in line. Then she'd hit him with a renegotiation. Either he gave her more of the empire she'd helped to build, or she walked.

Because she had the golden ticket—Elizabeth, heir to the fortune. As long as Nora had control of Merrell's offspring, then she had control of the wealth.

20

Nora lay stretched out on the terrace, soaking in the September sun.

September: the last month of her official mourning period.

Elizabeth, the golden ticket.

Those words had been circling Nora's brain since she first thought of them. She had control of Merrell's only child and with that came control of everything else. She just wasn't sure what that looked like yet.

Control.

She needed more of it.

A child's laugh filtered through the air and Nora heaved a sigh. She thought Raina and Elizabeth were gone.

From her spot in the back corner, Nora opened her eyes. She tilted up her wide-brimmed hat and gazed across the patio where Raina, Elizabeth, and another little girl played. The little girl laughed again, and Elizabeth responded with a tiny smile.

She'd barely muttered a word since Merrell's passing. Now here she was smiling as if her dad hadn't recently died.

Nora sat up. "Raina!"

Elizabeth froze. Raina jerked her head up. She scurried across the terrace. "I'm so sorry, Mrs. Hodges. I thought you were napping in your room."

"And I thought you were taking Elizabeth out for the afternoon."

Nervously, Raina shifted. "I-I was. That's my niece. She wanted to play on the beach. I brought them back here."

"I see." Nora lowered her sunglasses. "Well, obviously you're not playing on the beach. You're playing on my terrace."

Raina backed away. "I'll get them changed and down to the sand. I'm sorry."

"That's fine."

"Can I get you anything?"

"Cucumber water." *Control.* "Have Elizabeth bring it to me."

"Yes, ma'am."

Nora slid her sunglasses in place and stretched back out on the lounge chair. She closed her eyes and inhaled the salty breeze. Warm air blew past. Seagulls cawed. She breathed in, then out. There, that was more like it.

She felt more than heard Elizabeth's approach. Nora's eyes slit open to observe her daughter hesitantly placing cucumber water on the side table.

"Thank you, Elizabeth."

"I'm sorry if we disturbed your nap," she murmured.

"I'm sorry too. I'm so sad. I need lots of rest." Nora shifted, taking Elizabeth's stiff hand. "How are you, my daughter?"

Elizabeth hesitated. "Sad, too. I miss Daddy."

"That's good. You're supposed to be sad." Nora's fingers flexed around Elizabeth's hand. *Control.* "I want you to sleep with me tonight. You used to sleep with Daddy when he was sick. Raina told me how much it made him feel better. Well, I'm sad and that's like being sick. If you sleep with me, it'll make me feel better. Will you do that for me, Elizabeth?"

Her chin dipped in a single nod.

"Good girl."

Raina and her niece crossed over the terrace, heading to the beach. Elizabeth glanced over her shoulder. She turned to follow and Nora tightened her grip. Elizabeth turned back.

"Do you want to go play?" Nora asked.

"Yes."

Control. "Then, ask nicely."

Elizabeth hesitated.

Nora came up with a line that she instantly liked. "Mother, may I go play?"

"Mother, may I go play?" Elizabeth repeated.

Nora smiled. "Yes, you may." She released her hand and once again, settled back. She listened to her daughter shuffle away.

The golden ticket. Nora had it, and she would control it wisely.

21

That night Nora got ready for bed. She left the master suite and crossed the hall to Elizabeth's room.

Her daughter's voice filtered through the crack in the door. Nora crept up.

Elizabeth sat on the hand-knotted throw rug. Her Barbie dolls were scattered around. Off to the right towered a multilevel dollhouse taller than her daughter.

Carrying two dolls, she crawled over and placed a blond-haired Barbie on a chaise lounge. She'd already dressed the doll in navy silk pajamas.

Nora looked down at her own navy silk pajamas.

Next, Elizabeth put plaid shorts and a white tee on the other doll, this one smaller and with dark hair. She stood that one up next to the chaise.

She lifted the blond-haired doll's arm to point at the dark-haired one. "Elizabeth, you have been very, very bad. How many times do I have to tell you to be good? I'm so sad and you are selfish. You need to be better. I shouldn't have to remind you how to behave. If you would just behave, I wouldn't be so mean."

Elizabeth scooted the smaller one closer. "I'm sorry. Will you forgive me?"

"Yes, thank you for asking," the blonde one replied. "Now, give Mother a kiss on the cheek."

Elizabeth lifted the dark-haired one and pressed her face close to the blond-haired one. She imitated a kiss.

Nora watched, amused.

She opened the door and Elizabeth jerked around. Nora pretended she didn't see anything as she looked about the expansive room. A full-size canopy bed took up the corner with a pink and green comforter. A white wicker desk sat in front of the window and overlooked the ocean. On the desk was a state-of-the-art laptop. Beside it sat a small jewelry box that, when opened, revealed a ballerina dancing.

That's probably where she kept Hudson's necklace.

A walk-in closet led into a bathroom and back out into the main hall. Across the room, a tiny living room had been set up complete with pink and green bean bags and a flat-screen TV. The rest of the room contained cabinets and chests full of toys and clothes, all organized. By Raina or Elizabeth, Nora didn't know.

She stepped further into the room, pacing. "This is a little girl's room. Aren't you ready to graduate to a big girl's room? You'll be nine in a couple of months."

Elizabeth gathered her dolls and placed them neatly in a basket beside the dollhouse. "I like my room."

"Hm." Nora surveyed things a moment longer, then walked back to the door. "Let's go to bed."

Her daughter followed her to the master suite. Together they climbed into the king-size bed and settled under the sheets and blankets. Nora flipped off the light and rolled onto her side to see Elizabeth lying as far away as possible, staring up at the ceiling.

"This isn't how you slept with Daddy. You used to rest your head on his chest." Nora reached out. "Come here, Elizabeth. Hug me."

The blankets barely moved as her daughter slid across the mattress to deliver an awkward hug. As soon as Elizabeth's little arms went around Nora, she gripped her daughter tight.

Elizabeth tensed, but Nora kept hold. "If you would just behave, I wouldn't be so mean. Now, give Mother a kiss on the cheek."

At first, Elizabeth didn't move and Nora smiled to herself.

Then her daughter did, pressing a quick kiss, and Nora squeezed her tighter still. She didn't let go. She kept holding her until the minutes ticked to hours and her daughter finally drifted off.

Nora slid from the bed and tiptoed from the master suite.

22

The next morning, Elizabeth's scream echoed through the mansion.

At the kitchen table, Nora sipped her coffee.

Raina ran from the stove, sprinted through the downstairs, and took the steps three at a time to Elizabeth's room.

Nora flipped a page of the magazine she'd been reading.

Beyond the estate and out on the main road, a garbage truck beeped.

Minutes later, Elizabeth stepped into the kitchen, still dressed in her pajamas. Raina followed.

Nora glanced up, a pleasant smile on her face. "Good morning, daughter."

"Where are my things?" she whispered.

"Hm." Nora glanced at the clock. "Gone by now I suppose. I made sure to put a sign on the stack so the garbage people would know they could take it home and give it to their children." She looked at Elizabeth's red-rimmed eyes. "What's wrong? Have you been crying?"

"Why...why did you do that?"

"Do what?" Nora blinked.

"Give away my things."

"Oh." Nora frowned. "Well, I thought that's what you wanted. Last night we talked about it, remember? You said you were ready for a big girl's room."

Elizabeth didn't respond. She glanced over her shoulder at Raina, who looked just as distraught.

"Honestly, Elizabeth, most girls would be happy to redecorate." Nora stood up. "In fact, I've decided to redo the whole house. Now that Merrell's gone, we girls can make the place our own. A fresh start is good. It'll help us heal. It's not healthy to be surrounded by a dead person's things."

She crossed over to the coffee pot, poured another cup, and strolled past them. "Plus, you know how much he loved to donate to charity. I thought the gesture would make you happy. You had so many old things. Like the necklace Hudson gave you. It was time."

She floated up the steps and at the landing, she stopped to listen.

Elizabeth's quiet cries filtered up.

Nora sipped her coffee and disappeared into the master suite. Yes, redecorating would be great. She never liked Merrell's taste in coastal furniture. She preferred a more contemporary look.

Today she'd dive into Pinterest. She was all about a good mood board.

This would give her something to do until her mourning period was over.

23

Nora brought the calendar up on her phone. Three more days and she'd officially be done grieving Merrell's death.

Raina entered Nora's bedroom carrying a dry cleaning bag. Beneath the plastic hung a pink evening dress. In her other hand, she held a shoebox and coordinating handbag.

She laid it all on the bed. "This came for you."

Fragile and ravaged by cancer, Merrell laid in bed. "I'm too sick to attend," he said. "Will you go for me? Will you accept the award?"

"Of course." Nora touched his frail hand, trying not to show how excited she was.

A cough rattled his chest, followed by a weak smile. "Will you wear my favorite color?"

Nora had forgotten all about tonight's event.

She took a sip of her morning coffee, eyeing the pink monstrosity.

Her phone rang. A glance at the screen showed Cooper. "Yes?" she said.

"With everything that has happened, the Florida

Humanitarian Award being given tonight slipped my mind. The coordinator just called to ask who would be accepting in Merrell's place. I'll go and—"

"No. Before he died, Merrell asked me to. I told him I would. Let me go."

Cooper fell silent.

Nora rolled her eyes. "There's no ulterior motive." She simply wanted to be out of the house, surrounded by people, and back in the spotlight. Her Sunday and Wednesday appearances in church just weren't enough.

Plus, she wanted a new dress with accessories and a spa day. Okay, maybe there was an ulterior motive.

Still, silence.

"Good Lord, I'll be on my best behavior," she assured Cooper. "I won't bad-mouth Merrell for cutting me out of the will. Which, by the way, no one knows about, right?"

"Of course not. Just me and Hudson." He sighed. "Okay, it's in Miami. I've arranged for a car to drive you."

"One thing, though, Merrell wanted me to wear a pink evening gown. Obviously, that's not an appropriate color. I'll need a new black one. Given this is for Merrell, it shouldn't come from my allowance."

"Fine. Send me the receipts."

They hung up and Nora looked at Raina. "I'm going shopping. I'll also need a mani-pedi and a stylist. A massage too. I want to be relaxed. Things have been hard."

With a nod, Raina left and Nora took another sip of her coffee. She stood and stretched. Nothing like a little retail therapy and pampering to lift a girl's spirits.

THAT NIGHT, dressed in a black beaded-neck halter gown, Nora sat at her assigned table right up front in the banquet hall.

She applauded the woman who just won an award for some sort of work with dolphins. Nora didn't know, she was too busy admiring how her spray tan and manicure complemented the new black diamond ring that sparkled in the light.

The spray tan had been a last-minute idea as had the highlights. She'd opted for flat-ironed hair, her favorite, and a trim that brought it just to her shoulders. She loved the way the ends brushed her skin when she moved her head.

A glance at the program showed that was the final leadup. Next would be the big one—The Florida Humanitarian Award. Nora quickly freshened her lips with gloss.

The master of ceremonies approached the microphone. The banquet hall fell silent. He leaned in. "As the final award of this prestigious evening, we bestow our organization's highest accolade of humanitarianism upon a man known throughout the world, not only as a motivational speaker and man of God, but also as a generous soul held in high regard for his charitable, civic, and professional contributions. It is an honor to present this to a truly great man, Pastor Merrell Hodges."

The crowd applauded.

"With us tonight to accept the award on behalf of her recently deceased husband is Mrs. Nora Hodges." The master of ceremonies looked at Nora and she rose from the table.

She walked up the steps, crossing to the podium. She knew she looked stunning. Graciously, she accepted the crystal trophy with an amiable nod. A spotlight beamed on her and she rotated, making sure it picked up her beaded dress and black diamond drop earrings.

If she wasn't here tonight, she'd be at home on her third vodka by now. She needed this. It kept her on track.

"Thank you, ladies and gentlemen. It is a privilege to be here with you tonight and accept this honor on behalf of my late husband, Merrell Hodges. When I spoke with him about this night, he asked me to convey his dearest gratitude. He wanted so much to be here. I know he would want me to say 'Thank you' to every one of you who made this honor possible. On a more personal note, I'd like to say directly to him..." Nora took a long pause, sweeping her gaze across the audience.

Tears came to her eyes, one trailing perfectly down her cheek. With all her heart she said, "Congratulations, my love. I miss you dearly."

The crowd came to their feet. Nora sniffed and dabbed her cheek with the back of her hand. Could she conjure emotion or what?

24

Late the next morning, Nora walked into the kitchen to find Raina and Elizabeth looking at the crystal humanitarian award.

"It's beautiful," Elizabeth said to Raina.

"Yes, it is."

Nora looked at it without enthusiasm. "Put it in a box with his other things."

Carefully, Elizabeth curled her fingers around it and drew it close. "Thank you for going last night. I know how sad you've been and how hard the last few months have been on you." Her eyes shifted to Raina, who nodded.

Raina told Elizabeth to say that, but Nora didn't care. It left her speechless.

Sudden tears filled her eyes. Real tears, not the ones she conjured last night. She had a quick flash into the future where she saw her daughter as strong and capable and herself frail and weak.

It humbled her.

She slid around the kitchen island and hugged her daughter, holding tight. "Oh, Elizabeth. Thank you for saying that. No one has recognized how hard this has been for me."

Elizabeth didn't move.

Nora kept hugging her. "You know what I wish? I wish we could go back to when you were a toddler. You used to kiss me on the lips. It was the cutest thing. Do you remember?"

Silence.

"Do you remember?"

"Yes..."

"I love you." Nora kept hugging her.

More silence.

Nora pulled back to look into her daughter's brown eyes. "You rarely say those words to me. When you were teeny tiny, you said them all the time. I need to hear them. Can I hear them?"

"I love you."

Smiling, Nora kissed her daughter on the lips before reaching for the crystal humanitarian award. She drew on her inner strength and determination that made her life possible. "Really this belongs to me too. I helped Merrell with all that he did."

Clearing her throat, she straightened and held the award up, as if addressing the banquet hall from last night. "Thank you, ladies and gentlemen. It is a privilege to be here tonight and accept this honor. I'd like to dedicate it to my daughter, Elizabeth." Nora handed the crystal over. "I love you. I hope you know how much I mean that."

Silently, Elizabeth accepted the award.

25

In October, three months and one day after Merrell died, Nora requested a meeting with Cooper.

Dressed in her finest Alexander McQueen business suit, she drove her Mercedes into West Palm where Hodges Ministry was based.

The 600,000 square foot building was housed on seven acres of land. It contained classrooms, meeting areas, an administrative wing, a recording studio, the main sanctuary, a secondary sanctuary, a banquet hall, and a pre-school.

A plaque greeted her as she walked in.

> **WELCOME TO COVENANT GROVE CHURCH,**
> **HOME OF HODGES' MINISTRY.**
> **WE ARE A NON-DENOMINATIONAL ESTABLISHMENT.**
> **WE BELIEVE YOUR BEST DAYS ARE TO COME!**

A fond smile curved her lips as she remembered the day they broke ground. They both wore hard hats and grinned for the camera with their hands on a shovel. That picture hung in Merrell's office here at church.

Her heels clicked on the tile floor as she walked the length of the hall. The administrative area sat off to the right.

Two secretaries glanced up when she walked in. They both stood, big smiles on their faces.

"Mrs. Hodges!" One came around the desk to hug her. "You look fantastic. It's so good to see you here in the offices."

The other secretary hugged her as well.

"Thank you," Nora said with genuine gratefulness. She'd missed coming in for something other than church service or Bible study.

After a few more pleasantries, Nora left them. She crossed over and passed through double-glazed doors. To the right sat Merrell's old office and to the left, Cooper's. Straight ahead was Ferris Palmer, the junior pastor who had temporarily taken over the Sunday broadcast.

On the other side of the administration area were the offices of the staff who worked with community outreach, singles, couples, teen ministry, men's, women's, and kids groups.

The times Nora came in here, she always shared Merrell's space. He liked having her next to him. Now that office would be all hers.

She headed straight there, intending on putting her things away when Cooper appeared in his doorway. "Good morning."

She paused, catching a glimpse of herself in the ornamental mirror that hung above a hallway table. With the tailored suit, flat-ironed hair, and red lipstick, she looked beautiful, and she knew it. She felt twenty-five again.

Cooper surprised her with an embrace. "Why don't we chat in my office?"

He motioned her in and she slid into one of the two leather chairs situated in front of his gleaming wood desk. She placed her purse on the floor.

He sat behind his desk, leaning forward to brace his elbows on the freshly waxed top. "You look good."

She smiled. "Thank you. I'm excited to be back here in an official capacity."

He paused, seemingly thrown off by that.

"I was hoping we could discuss the future," she said. "I took over Merrell's travel while he was sick. Ferris has been doing the Sunday broadcast. I'm ready to step back in, be it the weekly broadcast, travel, a spot on the board—"

He cleared his throat.

She kept her smile in check. "What's wrong?"

"Ferris has been doing well. Better than expected. It's been over a year now since he stepped up to the plate. He's young and vibrant. His ratings are up. We did extensive focus groups. He's single, attractive, and a dynamic speaker. He's captured many hearts. He reminds me of Merrell." Cooper linked his fingers. "The board voted to promote him. He's the new Merrell Hodges."

Nora didn't pretend. The shock that hit her was real. "What are you talking about? When did this happen? Why am I just now hearing about it?"

"With Merrell's passing, we didn't want to bombard you. It became official a few days ago. I was going to tell you this weekend."

Her thoughts went in a million directions. "I...I helped build this place. My name is on the building. I'm the face people expect to see. I don't understand how this is happening. I've been here every Sunday since Merrell died. Every Wednesday too. The board has to know how much I want to stay involved. Do they not know that?"

"Of course you can stay involved. We have all kinds of volunteer projects we need help on."

"Volunteer projects?"

Cooper sighed. His voice came quiet and gentle. "People were ready for a change."

Nora's jaw tightened.

That's when she saw it—a new plaque—propped in the corner of Cooper's office. It still had cellophane wrapped around it.

> *Welcome to Covenant Grove Church.*
> *We are a non-denominational establishment.*
> *We believe your best days are to come!*

Nora exploded to her feet. "This is all your fault. You made me into his 'arm candy.' You never saw my potential." Sudden tears filled her eyes. "You always saw me as that white trashy girl that Merrell fell in love with. I could've been great, but I always took the back seat to Merrell and 'God's calling.'"

"Listen to me, Nora. Listen with your logic and not your pride. I never underestimated you. Merrell is the man he became because of you. The two of you together were Christian royalty. You are a gorgeous, intelligent woman. But things change. At least here they have. Nothing is keeping you from starting over, and you're certainly welcome here to attend service."

"Oh, am I? Am I *welcome* to attend service at the church I started?" She huffed an unamused laugh. "I don't want to start over. I want this." She jabbed her finger on the top of his desk. "I built this empire. I deserve the spotlight. You are going to be so sorry that you didn't let me take over Merrell's ministry."

"It's the board's decision."

"Oh, bullshit." She leaned forward. "Tell me. Why did Merrell leave his estate to Elizabeth?"

"I don't know. He wouldn't tell me." Cooper lowered his voice. "It's time for a change, Nora. Move on. Prove yourself without Merrell."

Her body shook. Nora sat back down. Embarrassment heated her cheeks. "I sacrificed my whole life for that man and this is what I get as a thank-you."

Cooper fell silent.

"Does everyone know?" she whispered.

"We made a staff announcement that you're taking time to yourself and that you're grateful for Ferris' willingness to step in."

She supposed she should be grateful Cooper worded it that way, but there was nothing grateful about this situation. Wiping her eyes, she stood back up. She straightened her shoulders, and like a great athlete, she found the strength for one last push. She held her head high. "Please box up Merrell's office and have it delivered to my home."

"Will do." Cooper walked around his desk and over to the office door. Before he opened it he said, "As the manager of Elizabeth's estate, I have to remind you to run things by me. You can't redecorate without clearing it with me first. Normal things are fine—groceries, clothes, incidentals—but redecorating a 17,000 square foot home isn't considered an incidental."

Whatever.

He opened the door. "Goodbye, Nora."

She slid her purse over her shoulder and as she walked from the office, she ran into Ferris Palmer, the new Merrell.

Tall and lean with auburn hair and blue eyes, he smiled kindly. "Nora." He hugged her. "So good to see you."

Nora fought the angry tears. "Yes, good to see you as well." Ferris took a step back and she fastened a brave smile. "Thank you for stepping up. Merrell would be proud."

"That's generous of you. I thought the world of Merrell. He was my mentor but I considered him a father figure as well."

"He would have liked knowing that." Nora squeezed his hand, offered a nod to Cooper, then continued on.

Out in the main area, the two secretaries smiled as Nora left. In the hall, a janitor waved. She waved back. Outside a family was walking in and they stopped to say hi.

Finally, in her car, Nora gripped the wheel and closed her eyes. She took a deep breath. She counted to ten. With a set jaw, she started the Mercedes. A car pulled in a few slots away. Nora didn't want to smile and wave. She pretended not to see them as she backed out and drove slowly along the drive.

She felt exiled.

Because she was.

26

Nora drove for hours. Morning transitioned to the afternoon. The afternoon moved into night. Her Mercedes headed south along A1A to the Keys.

She considered renting a room and staying forever.

She thought about buying a plane ticket to anywhere.

She looked at chartering a boat and disappearing.

That's when she remembered Merrell's antique sailboat. His "me" time. God, she hated that thing.

He'd bought the fixer-upper nearly ten years ago and spent ridiculous amounts of time tinkering with it. He stripped it, sanded it, and repainted it. He gutted the insides and scoured the internet for replacement parts. It took him five years to restore it.

Like any good "arm candy," Nora oohed and aahed instead of rolling her eyes. Why couldn't he just buy a yacht like any other multimillionaire in Palm Beach? No, not Merrell. He had to restore a stupid wood boat.

She went sailing with him exactly one time and was so bored she visualized jumping over and drowning. She feigned seasickness to get out of any other future trips.

When Elizabeth was a toddler, he took her out on the eighteen-foot boat. She came home afterward, babbling with excitement. She couldn't wait to go out again. At the time, Nora had been glad. Merrell now had a sailing buddy.

Now, Nora wanted it demolished.

She pulled into her driveway at midnight and left her car running as she charged inside and went straight upstairs. She walked past the master suite and into Elizabeth's room. She grabbed her arm and tugged her from the bed.

Elizabeth stumbled after her, hovering between wake and sleep. Nora dragged her down the steps and out the front door. She opened the passenger side of the Mercedes and shoved her in. "Buckle up."

She crossed over to the gardening shed, grabbed an ax, and put it in the trunk. Her tires squealed as she drove away.

She steered the car across town. The farther she got from their estate, the more Elizabeth woke up. When they neared the marina, her daughter was clutching the seat and staring wide-eyed out the front window.

To the left sat the wet slips and to the right the dry dock. Nora went right. She pulled down the length of boats in various stages of repair to the back where Merrell's restored antique sat on its trailer.

She left the car running with the headlights focused on the boat. They cast pale shafts in the pitch black.

Nora retrieved the ax from the trunk. Her blood boiled as she swung it overhead and delivered the first whack. It made a satisfying crack into the polished wood.

She swiveled the ax back to the left and came up and under the hull. Gleaming planks splintered into two chunks.

Tightening her grip, she shifted to the right and did

another overhand straight down on the bow. Another crack reverberated through the air.

Sweat gathered in her cleavage. She rounded the boat. The ax connected with the wood. A large section broke loose.

Nora laughed.

She continued hacking. The blade attacked in a methodical disjointed and satisfying beat. More large chunks broke loose.

The skin on her hands began to rub raw and bleed. She ignored them as she circled the sailboat with vicious blows.

Her breathing increased. Her pulse pumped. She paused and looked around the area, spying a sledgehammer propped against another vessel several yards away.

She whirled to face the Mercedes. The headlights blinded her as she looked through the windshield at Elizabeth and pointed to the sledgehammer. "Bring me that."

The passenger door opened. Nora turned away to savagely attack another section.

"Goddamned men," she muttered. "They don't give a holy hell about anyone but themselves. I gave my whole life and I have nothing to show for it."

Elizabeth drug the sledgehammer over and Nora paused long enough to switch from the ax to the hammer. The heavy head connected with the wood in a powerful and loud thunk. It flattened the already splintered pieces.

She smiled and advanced to the next section. She caught sight of her daughter standing a careful distance away, paralyzed with terror.

Sweat slicked Nora's face. Still dressed in her expensive business suit, the fabric stuck to her skin. She didn't care. All she cared about was demolishing the boat.

When the sledgehammer got too heavy, she yelled, "Bring me the ax again!"

Elizabeth hurriedly retrieved it.

Panting, Nora studied the antique sailboat, now a pile of splintered wood. She zeroed in on the last part and didn't hesitate to take the ax and finish the job.

Elizabeth watched in horror but Nora ignored her frightened child. She chopped away until the boat toppled inward. She wished she had a flame thrower.

When the last few pieces broke, she stood triumphantly, surveying the havoc.

A job well done.

She put the ax back in the trunk, told Elizabeth to get in, and drove home with bloody hands and a torn three-thousand-dollar business suit.

It was exactly what she needed.

27

Once again Nora found herself dialing her mama.

"You get out ahead of this," Mama said. "You let everyone know you're in full support of that Ferris Palmer boy. I didn't raise no idiot. You know rich people now. Take advantage of that. Merrell did you wrong. It's your turn now. I'm gonna email you something I read recently." Her mama laughed. "You decide to do it, and it'll be the ultimate middle finger to that dead husband of yours."

An hour later the email came in. The subject line read: NO ONE WILL EVER KNOW

> In the wake of tragedies large and small, they pop up like mushrooms after a rain. With tales of woe and heartbreaking images of children or helpless animals, they beg for assistance. They are the tragi-charities. One-hit wonders seeking to cash in on the tragedy of the day from floods and fires to missing children and more.
>
> The pop-up charity business is usually local, occasionally regional, and rarely national. Mostly they are the

products of individual scammers who smell an opportunity to cash in using the name of a victim who may or may not even be real. They count on local press coverage and a quick website. These "charities" usually rake in a few thousand dollars and disappear.

Then there are the professional **long term operations**. They utilize **wealthy associates**, direct mail, or telemarketers to solicit **millions of dollars** in donations from unsuspecting individuals and businesses.

The percentages spent by these "charities" on direct aid to victims range from 0% to a **high of only 11.10%**. This is a far cry from what well-meaning contributors intended for their contributions.

When a solicitor for one of these groups calls a prospective donor the pitch will include the truthful statement that they are a nonprofit organization. **Nonprofit however does not mean they are a charity.** It only means they do not seek to make a profit on their activities. A charity is only one type of nonprofit.

Lots of different special interest groups are nonprofits, including some private businesses **that pay their executives quite well.**

The article that was taken from the website *SmartAsset* continued. Nora read and reread every word. She noted the items her mama had placed in bold lettering. With a smirk, she got a notebook and pen and charted a plan.

28

November moved in and with it, milder Florida temperatures. Nora glided down the steps of her home. The chatter of women filled her living room. Ten ladies in all—some from church and others from the community—here by invitation for a luncheon.

They all knew each other already. Nora made sure of that when she devised the guest list.

Their ages ranged from thirty-something to seventy-something. Some were married and others single. Some had children and others had none. Some worked and others didn't. But they all had one thing in common.

Money.

Dressed in a white silk-linen pantsuit, Nora made her grand entrance. The women stood to greet her. Hugs were exchanged and kisses on the cheek.

"How lovely you look."

"How are you holding up?"

"I love what you did with the place."

"I've been meaning to stop by."

"How is Elizabeth?"

"I saw you in church last Sunday..."

Nora smiled through it all, waiting to speak. She motioned everyone to sit back down. "It's ladies like you who make my day possible. I depend on my support system. Thank you for coming." She spied the gift someone had brought—a platinum rose and tree of life vase—and sighed. Now that was a good gift. "Oh my goodness. That is gorgeous."

"It's from all of us," Mrs. Morgan said. She was seventy-five and married to a financial advisor.

Nora looked around the group. "I've missed this so much." She glanced over to a side table where she'd placed the photo of her and Merrell breaking ground at church. She'd put it back in a box after the ladies left. Now, though, she conjured tears. "Other than going to church each week, I haven't been getting out. It's been hard."

They murmured their understanding.

She sniffed back the tears, putting on a brave face. "Your love and support mean the world to me. Thank you."

Nora allowed a beat to go by as she made eye contact with each of them. They gazed back in admiration and emotion. Another sniff. She shook her head and waved her hand. "Enough of this. How about lunch? Raina has put on a spread."

The ladies moved into the formal dining room where a long table had been set with seashell themed china. Nora had Raina position the table at an angle so every lady had a view of the terrace and the Atlantic Ocean.

She stood proudly at the head, motioning everyone to find their name cards. Conversation buzzed as Raina circled to place platters throughout. Nora had put an extensive menu together with a vintage theme including various salads, fizzy drinks, quiche, canapes, sautéed radishes, olives, almond wraps, and a few other items.

The ladies complimented her on the variety and everyone enjoyed the meal.

It was ten minutes in when someone spied Elizabeth on the terrace. "Oh, my... she is getting so big. How old is she now?"

"She'll be nine next month," Nora said.

The room quieted as everyone gazed out the floor-to-ceiling windows at Elizabeth playing near the pool.

"She looks so much like her father," someone quietly said and everyone murmured in agreement.

Nora waved Raina over. Seeing as how her daughter had stolen the show, might as well bring her in. "Has Elizabeth eaten?" Nora asked Raina.

"Not yet."

"Set a plate. Let her eat with us."

The ladies smiled, loving that idea and everyone went back to their food. The conversation once again buzzed and five minutes later Elizabeth was seated beside Nora.

All focus went to her.

"What have you been doing?"

"What's your favorite subject in school?"

"Do you realize how much you look like your daddy?"

The questions came and Elizabeth answered. She made jokes and they laughed. She spoke like someone years older. She had a natural way about her, just like Merrell.

Nora didn't recognize this friendly and personable little girl. Elizabeth never acted this way around her.

She took it personally.

"Eat your food, Elizabeth." Nora tapped her daughter's plate.

Elizabeth's nose crinkled. "It's too fancy."

The ladies chuckled.

"It's not too fancy." Nora kept her smile in check. "Eat your food, please. Don't be picky."

"No, thank you." Elizabeth placed her hands in her lap. "I'm not hungry."

Still, with her smile, Nora looked around the faces of her company. "I'm sure Elizabeth is bored with all this adult stuff. We'll let her get back to playing."

The ladies were disappointed but they understood. Soon, Elizabeth was back outside playing. Nora instructed Raina to put her daughter's uneaten plate on the kitchen table. The luncheon continued. Eventually, they moved back into the living room for coffee.

The moment had come, and Nora shared a generous smile with the women. "Ladies, my heart is full and warm after today. I'm so pleased you came. I asked you here because I've missed this, girl time, but also because I wanted to announce something. I have decided to open a non-profit in Merrell's name. He loved children and we spoke often about adoption. But then he got sick..." Nora paused, working up a tear.

She dabbed her eye and sniffed. "I've taken a million dollars and opened The Merrell Hodges Foundation to protect homeless children. I would be honored to have you wonderful and generous ladies involved. There is no obligation or pressure. Just know I would be honored."

Of course, she didn't open it with a million dollars. She used one hundred to make it legal and on the books.

Their faces lit and Nora knew she had them.

Mrs. Morgan didn't hesitate. She pulled a checkbook out of her purse and wrote a sizable amount to the foundation. Another elderly lady did the same. Some of the younger women who didn't carry checkbooks asked for routing information. Nora had printed cards with the foundation details and had them ready to hand out.

By the end of the week, she expected the deposits to come rolling in. She expected the word to spread. If everything went according to plan, she'd have that million in donations. Ten percent would go to some children's organization and the rest would roll right back into the overhead, aka Nora's pocketbook.

In a few months, she'd repeat this with a new guest list. More word would spread. The possibilities were endless. She'd be accepting that humanitarian award. She'd soon be Nora Hodges, the philanthropist. There'd be charity balls. Media coverage. World tours as she branched out to needy children abroad.

Yes, the possibilities were endless.

The afternoon with the women came to a close. Goodbyes were exchanged. She saw them to the door.

While Raina cleaned, Nora drove to the closest store and bought a bag of dry dog food. She returned home and walked into the kitchen. She poured a bowl of dog food and set it on the kitchen table next to the plate of Elizabeth's uneaten food.

She retrieved her daughter who was now in her bedroom and put her at the kitchen table. Elizabeth eyed the dog food and the plate of uneaten human food that had begun to congeal.

Nora sat down across from her. "When I was your age, my mama worked at a tiny little country store. Every day I rode the school bus and got off at that store. I did my homework. I stocked shelves. I bagged groceries. For dinner every night I ate the same thing—Vienna sausages and saltine crackers. It was all my mama could afford. One night I pushed it away. I didn't want to eat it. I was being picky. So,

Mama opened a bag of dog food and poured me a bowl. She said I could either eat the dog food or the sausages. My choice. I chose the sausages."

She nodded to the bowl of dog food in front of Elizabeth. "I am now giving you that choice. I will not have a picky daughter. You can either eat that plate of 'fancy' food or you can have that bowl of dog food. Your choice. You will not leave this table until one of those actions occur."

Nora stood up. "You were disobedient in front of my friends. That embarrassed me. I expect an apology."

Elizabeth folded her arms and glared.

"Fine, be a brat. I'll accept your apology later." Nora walked past Raina, ignoring her shocked face. She said, "If she leaves that table, you're fired. Just so we're clear, that means you immediately move out of the garage apartment, you never see Elizabeth again, and I tip off immigration that you're in this country illegally."

29

Early evening light slanted across Elizabeth's face from a nearby window. She sat alone at the kitchen table, staring at the items in front of her. On the right was the bowl of dog food and on the left the plate of hours-old human food.

Nora hovered just outside the doorway, watching her stubborn little girl.

She allowed a few moments to go by before entering the kitchen. She put ice in a glass, poured a generous amount of vodka, and dropped a wedge of lime on top. She sipped it as she walked over to the kitchen table.

Elizabeth didn't look up.

"Do you need to use the bathroom?" Nora asked.

Her daughter nodded.

"You may get up and do that. Come right back."

Slowly, Elizabeth walked from the kitchen and into the downstairs bathroom. Nora sipped more vodka.

She heard the toilet flush and the water run. Then her daughter returned to take her seat.

Nora turned off the kitchen light and left her there.

As she was walking upstairs, she ran into Raina. "She'll sleep in that kitchen if need be."

"Yes, ma'am," Raina mumbled.

∼

At two in the morning, Nora quietly walked from the master suite. She took the steps down, crossed through the foyer, and into the kitchen. Elizabeth had pushed the items away and laid her head down on the table. She slept soundly, her breaths coming even and deep.

Nora glided across the tile floor. She stood beside the corner table, eyeing the dog food and the plate of untouched human food with dried out cheese, limp lettuce, and the sautéed radishes congealed in butter.

"What am I going to do with you?" she whispered. "You are something else. I would've given in by now."

Elizabeth shifted, slowly waking up.

She lifted her head and when her eyes locked with Nora's, she straightened up.

Nora said, "You will sit here all day tomorrow as well."

Elizabeth didn't blink. She didn't speak. She simply folded her arms and looked away.

"Fine. But don't try throwing it away or putting it down the garbage disposal. I'll know." Nora once again walked from the kitchen.

∼

At seven in the morning, Raina tapped on Nora's bedroom door. The fear in her voice came raw and palpable when she said, "Elizabeth is gone."

Nora drove slowly along Ocean Boulevard. Nervously she peered up and down the street lined with multimillion-dollar estates. What if someone had found Elizabeth and taken her in? What if they'd called the cops? How would Nora explain this?

She'd tell the truth. She'd say they had a mother-daughter spat and Elizabeth ran off. Anybody with a child would understand that explanation.

Up ahead, she spied a slender dark-haired girl and sped up. She was just about to slam her hand on the horn when the little girl's father walked from behind a palm tree with a poodle on a leash.

Nora's fingers tightened around the wheel. Her teeth ground. She steered her Mercedes north.

Moments later, a woman out for a morning jog glanced over and waved. Nora forced herself to smile and wave back.

She accelerated past, still searching.

Elizabeth had it coming, that was for sure.

Nora drove the entire length of the boulevard. The sun rose over the ocean. Forty-five minutes ticked by. At the end of the road, she turned the car around and pulled over to the side.

She closed her eyes and breathed.

But the more she breathed, the more her irritation transitioned into worry. Elizabeth had never run away from home. If she was trying to prove a point, then point proven. Nora had taken things too far.

What was she going to do?

Honestly, she just wanted her daughter back. She wouldn't make her choose between the bowl and the plate.

She'd throw both away as soon as they got home. She promised.

This was all her mama's fault. Nora would have never had the dog food idea if not for Mama. There were other ways to handle a picky and disobedient child.

She'd made a mistake.

She was about to call Raina to see if Elizabeth had returned when Nora caught sight of her daughter walking over a dune toward the ocean.

The driver's door flew open and still dressed in her pajamas, Nora sprinted toward her. "Elizabeth!" she cried.

Her daughter glanced up and froze.

In the flip flops that she'd hurriedly slipped on, Nora climbed the dune. She came down on her knees and grabbed her daughter's shoulders. "Oh, Elizabeth." She drew her into a hug. "I was so scared. You worried me sick."

Real tears filled Nora's eyes as she pulled away. She inspected Elizabeth, reassuring herself that she was okay. Nora smiled in relief, but Elizabeth didn't smile back.

"This is the worst place to pull a runaway act. What if someone saw?" She gathered her daughter back into a tight embrace.

A few seconds ticked by.

Why wasn't Elizabeth hugging her back?

She released her grip, once again gazing at her daughter's unreadable expression. "It's for your own good, the things I do. I know you think I'm mean. I had it hard growing up. Nothing like you have it. Look where you live. Look at the things you have."

Her daughter glanced down at the sand and Nora studied the crown of her dark hair. Maybe she should send her to live with Mama. Elizabeth would appreciate her own mother then.

She was about to say as much when she caught sight of the woman jogger from earlier. The woman didn't wave or smile but instead cast a disapproving look.

"We know we're on the dune," Nora called out. "We'll get off."

Putting her arm around Elizabeth, she led her down the sandy hill. At the bottom, she stopped and knelt back down. She tried to catch her daughter's eyes but Elizabeth wouldn't look at her.

"Are you hungry?" Nora quietly asked.

"Yes." Tears filled Elizabeth's eyes, and she was happy to see them. Maybe her daughter did feel bad about being disobedient and running away.

"What do you say we throw all that stuff away and have Raina make pancakes? How does that sound?"

The tears in Elizabeth's eyes tipped over to trail her cheeks. She nodded, finally making eye contact.

"I love you, daughter. I hope you know that." Nora paused. "Tell me you know that."

Carefully, her daughter nodded.

"Will you tell me you love me, too? Mothers need to hear that."

Elizabeth hesitated.

"Please?"

"I love you, too," Elizabeth whispered.

A relieved smile curved her face. "Now, give Mother a kiss on the cheek." She tilted her cheek and Elizabeth quickly obliged.

Holding her daughter's hand, she led her to the Mercedes. When they reached the passenger side, she stopped and looked down at Elizabeth. "Are you ready to go home?"

Her daughter nodded.

"Then, ask nicely."

Elizabeth swallowed and for a second, Nora wasn't sure if she'd oblige. Then quietly, she spoke. "Mother, may I come home?"

"Yes, you may."

30

November rolled into December. The Merrell Hodges Foundation hosted the annual children's Christmas event. As with every other year, the Christian Television Network covered it as well as local media.

Elizabeth turned nine.

January transitioned to February. Nora held another luncheon at her home. The donations rolled in.

March turned to April. Nora made a very public donation to the Florida Coalition for Homeless Children. She also bought a new wardrobe.

May transitioned to June. *Forbe's* "The 20 Most Charitable Women of the Year" came out and Nora made #20, right under Jada Pinkett Smith. Next year she'd hit #1 and beat out Oprah.

July moved into August and the money continued to flow in without Nora doing a single thing. She showed her gratitude by giving 10 percent back. She also treated herself to a much-anticipated vacation to Italy.

In September she attended the Humanitarian Awards

where she received the same honor that Merrell had received the previous year. She felt pride in possessing a crystal trophy etched with her name, not Merrell's. She also bought a jet.

Every Sunday she attended church, sitting in the front with Elizabeth and Raina, right where the cameras would see her. She received more TV time than Ferris Palmer.

He wasn't doing as well as everyone had hoped.

Mama would say Nora was living her best life. But Nora wanted more. She wanted Merrell's job and Ferris demoted back to where he belonged.

On a Sunday in October, Cooper approached her after church. "You seem to be doing well."

"I am, thank you."

"The Merrell Hodges Foundation is thriving."

"Yes, it is." Nora smiled to mask her smirk. At the rate she was going, she'd have equal to that of Merrell's estate within the next year. Imagine what she could do after that.

Cooper said, "I'm sure you're aware of the podcast Ferris has been doing."

"Yes, of course."

"What are your thoughts on being a guest?"

Nora kept her smile in check. She knew Cooper well enough to know that this was his way of feeling her out on the possibilities of more. "I'd be honored. Thank you. I'll have to check my schedule. It's quite full these days."

Cooper kept his smile in check as well. "Whatever time you can give us would be great, Nora."

She waited for a beat. "Let's cut to the chase. Ferris isn't doing well. You and I both know that. I want Merrell's job. Put Ferris back as junior pastor. Give me the weekly televised broadcast."

He didn't blink. "Actually, the board has been talking about that."

She wasn't surprised. She also knew how much Cooper liked a good negotiation, so she said, "I'll do the podcast. I will promise you a top ten slot for the week. When that happens, the board will give me a co-pastor slot. After a suitable amount of time, that co-slot will become singular with Ferris being moved back down to the junior position. I will get Merrell's old office. My salary will equal Merrell's for the first year with a ten percent increase after that. Ferris can keep the podcast. That's a non-issue for me." She blinked because he still hadn't. "Agreed?"

"Agreed."

31

The first Monday in November, Nora sat opposite Ferris Palmer in the church studio with headphones on and a microphone in front of her.

"Nora Hodges," Ferris said. "I am delighted to have you on my show."

"Thank you," she spoke into the microphone. "I am pleased to be here."

She'd read the script and was already prepared to interrupt.

"Love is today's topic," Ferris said, glancing at the lines Cooper had given both of them. "The Bible says we are to love one another—"

"But what if we can't stand someone?" She glanced at Cooper who sat quietly in the corner.

His eyes narrowed.

"Um..." Ferris looked between them.

Good, this was exactly what she wanted. She picked up the pages Cooper had given her and turned them over on the table in front of her. Listeners reacted best to unrehearsed and off-the-cuff discussions. It made for better flow.

Cooper wanted the ratings up and the magic back? This would do it.

She reached across the table and turned Ferris's over too.

Let's just talk, she mouthed.

He looked over his shoulder at Cooper. Ferris may need his approval, but Nora didn't. "Love," she said. "That's hard to do. Because people can be irritating. Am I right? It's easy to say 'I'm so glad you're a part of the family of God' when what you're really thinking is 'I'm surprised you're a part of the family of God!'"

"Oh goodness." Ferris laughed.

That's right, she wasn't the hot-rolled, made up, perfectly spoken woman Merrell always wanted and Cooper portrayed. She was done with that phase of her life. Cooper planned to put her back up on that stage? Then he needed to know this was who he would get.

And by God, they would stop relying on Cooper's surveys and polls and focus groups.

"Love," she said again. "What are the ways it can be shown? Do we wear Christian T-shirts? Do we have a cross around our neck? Do we drive around with a 'Honk if you love Jesus' bumper sticker?"

Ferris chuckled. "I do have one of those on my car."

Of course, he did.

"It's hard enough loving our own family. Or those you've known so long they're like family." She looked pointedly at Cooper.

He shook his head, warning her not to take it too far. That's fine. She knew when to rein it in.

Ferris turned the script back over. "Everything we do should pass through a filter of love, or it means nothing at all," he read.

No wonder his ratings had dipped. He didn't have his own thoughts.

"What we need to ask ourselves is why? I don't know about you, but I have to understand the importance of a word before it settles in. 'Love one another as I have loved you.' Logic says if you love your spouse you won't commit adultery. If you love your mother you won't lie. If you love your enemy, you won't harbor a desire to hurt him. If you love your child you won't abuse them…" Her voice trailed off with her thoughts. She sat back in her chair. Her brow furrowed.

Ferris stared at her, but when he realized she wasn't going to say anything, he quickly referenced his notes again.

Abruptly, she sat forward. "God developed people who reflected his character." Her head shook. "No, let me rephrase that. It was his plan to do that. But there is free will and temptation that lead some off the path…" Nora paused for a beat, thinking over the words she'd just said. "'The Devil made me do it,'" she murmured.

Ferris's brow furrowed.

"I suppose there's something to that, yeah? The good ole Devil. What's important, though, is realizing your wrong-doing and then getting back on the path of love."

"How does that work?" he asked.

"It's simple. You ask for forgiveness and try again…" Once again her focus trailed off. So many people needed to ask for Nora's forgiveness—Hudson, Cooper, Mama, Merrell, too, if he could come back from the grave.

"Love is a warm and wonderful feeling," Ferris said with a dreamy smile.

Just what she needed, a romantic. "Love is also confused by lust and gratification."

Ferris's eyes popped wide.

"What? We're all human. I've lusted. I've experienced gratification. I've sinned. There is nothing wrong with admitting that."

"No, I suppose not," Ferris hesitantly agreed.

"However, this is a discussion on love, not sin." She laughed. "We'll tackle sin another day. Love is vulnerable. It exposes the heart. Imagine opening yours and receiving ridicule in response?"

Ferris nodded. "As Jesus did. He opened his heart, only to have it broken. But he forgave."

Forgave.

Had she forgiven Hudson for leaving her that night in the hotel? Had she forgiven Merrell for cutting her out of the will? Had she forgiven her mama for her whole life? Would she ever?

Not when getting even sounded much better.

"Love entails a cost. It takes a chance. It does the unexpected. It leaves an impression." Yes, Nora liked the thought of getting even much better than forgiveness.

In the corner, Cooper held up a Bible, reminding the two of them to work in verses.

Ferris immediately referenced his lines. "John one-eleven says..."

The podcast continued another twenty minutes until Cooper motioned to wrap things up.

Ferris finished, once again reading from the script that Cooper had given both of them. "In the end, there is hope for anyone who has failed to love. The Lord is standing by ready to forgive you for your lack of love. He's ready to show you mercy and to cleanse your loveless heart."

There is hope for anyone who has failed to love.

Was their hope for Mama? Nora didn't think so. Her mama had never and would never ask for forgiveness. Nora wished she felt indifferent, but she didn't. She cared what her mama thought.

Hudson, though, was another story.

The studio light flipped from red to green, indicating they were no longer live. Cooper didn't say a word, he simply walked from the room. She didn't care. She knew it went well.

Ferris grinned. "That was fun!"

If this was his idea of fun, he needed to get out more.

Ferris walked her out to her Mercedes, they said goodbye, and as Nora drove away, she didn't think of Mama, Hudson, or Merrell. She thought of the word love as it related to Elizabeth.

They rarely spoke. They seldom hugged. Elizabeth never said *I love you* unless Nora requested it.

They simply did not like each other.

As much as Nora hated to admit it, their relationship mirrored the one she shared with her mama. If they were going to get back on track, they needed to talk. Nora wanted to like her daughter. She wanted to love her.

She just didn't know how.

32

When Nora arrived home, Raina and Elizabeth sat across from each other at the kitchen table listening to the podcast. Her daughter stared at the speaker in fascination. Nora stayed out of sight, listening as well. She felt pleased that her voice filtered through with relatable emotion. It was exactly how she wanted to come across.

Ferris's voice finished with, "In the end, there is hope for anyone who has failed to love. The Lord is standing by ready to forgive you for your lack of love. He's ready to show you mercy and to cleanse your loveless heart."

The air in the kitchen fell silent.

"What did you think?" Raina asked.

"Do you think Mother believes all of that?" Elizabeth quietly said.

Raina sighed. "I think your mother is conflicted. She didn't have an easy life until she met your daddy. She's sometimes hard on you because she doesn't know how else to be. She loves you very much but isn't always sure how to show it. You don't understand this, but she's had to start over since your daddy died. That takes a very brave person. You should be proud of her."

Nora couldn't have said it any better.

Elizabeth thought about that. "Okay, I will. I'll be proud of her."

Nora picked that moment to make her appearance. Raina glanced up. "We just listened to the podcast, Mrs. Hodges. You did great."

"Thank you." Nora looked at Elizabeth. "What did you think?"

"Yes." Her daughter nodded. "I'm proud of you."

Nora's heart swelled with love. "I haven't told anyone yet, because I didn't want to jinx it. If this podcast hits the top ten slot, I'll be doing the weekly televised show again."

"You'll get it," Raina said. "I know it."

∾

NORA DIDN'T SLEEP. Every hour she checked the podcast. Reviews climbed. So did downloads and plays. Her hopes rose.

Top fifty.

Forty.

Thirty.

Twenty.

By five in the morning, she paced the kitchen, praying for the top ten slot. Her phone sat powered up and ready on the island. Cooper was an early riser. As soon as it hit top ten, he'd call.

An hour later Raina walked into the kitchen. "Oh, Mrs. Hodges! I didn't know you were up. Can I make you something?"

Nora waved her off. "I'm too nervous to eat." She allowed

herself one more cup of coffee. She launched the podcast app to discover more reviews, downloads, and plays, now putting it in the top fifteen.

Five more to go.

At seven, Elizabeth shuffled into the kitchen. She stopped and looked between Raina and Nora. "What's going on?"

"I'm waiting to hit the top ten slot." She checked the app. She'd only dropped one slot to fourteen.

The lights and shadows shifted as the sun rose further over the ocean.

Raina handed Elizabeth cranberry juice. Even though Nora didn't ask for it, Raina served her a sweet potato with almond butter instead of peanut butter.

Elizabeth was in the kitchen, otherwise Nora would get what she preferred.

Her daughter climbed onto a barstool near Nora's phone. She sipped her juice and stared at it.

Nora tightened her thin robe as she paced the kitchen. She switched from coffee to herbal tea. She took a bite of her sweet potato. No one spoke. Anticipation clung to the air.

She checked the app. Two more slots put her at twelve.

Raina toasted bread and smeared avocado on it. She slid the plate across the island to Elizabeth. She took one bite as Nora had of her breakfast, then she went back to staring at the phone.

Nora breathed out, considering a shot of vodka.

She checked the ratings. Top eleven. Her heart paused beating. One more to go.

Nora grabbed her phone. "Should I call Cooper? It's at eleven. It's going to hit ten. I know it." She looked between Raina and Elizabeth. "It will hit ten, right?"

"Of course," Raina said, not hesitating.

With a nod, Nora paced a tight circle.

"It's going to be okay," Elizabeth told her. "Any second now it'll hit top ten."

Nora stopped pacing. She breathed out. "You are so sweet."

Her phone rang. She froze. Cooper's name lit up the screen. She put both hands over her heart. It rang again. She answered. "Cooper? Good morning."

"Congratulations, Nora. You are currently at number 9 and expected to go to number 1."

She wanted to scream in his ear. *Yes! Yes! Yes!* But she managed to stay in control. "That's wonderful. Thank you for the fabulous news."

"We'll need to discuss the next steps, but enjoy the celebration today and I'll be in touch."

They clicked off and Nora flung her arms into the air. "Yes!"

Raina laughed. "Wonderful!"

Nora tugged Elizabeth off the stool and danced her across the kitchen. She hugged her and kissed her and let go to do the same with Raina.

Giggling, Nora skipped out of the kitchen and into the foyer. She looked at herself in a wall-mounted gold-flecked mirror. The smile that came was real and it felt great. It had been too long since she had a genuine smile.

At this moment she saw her future spreading endlessly with hard-earned and honest opportunity, not manufactured like The Merrell Hodges Foundation. She drank the moment in, feeling as if heaven radiated through her.

She imagined a packed arena cheering for her as she humbly nodded her acceptance of their love. She opened her arms and bowed with a modest thank-you. She blew a kiss.

Then she laughed at her silliness.

When she turned from the mirror, Raina and Elizabeth stood side by side staring at her.

She probably looked ridiculous, but Nora didn't care. She hugged herself and spun a circle, giggling with victorious glee.

Then she took off upstairs. Now was the perfect time to see Hudson Davis.

33

Nora had no clue if Hudson was home. But she drove into West Palm where he kept a condo near his office.

As she had done many times before, she pulled into the underground garage and parked in a guest spot. She keyed in the code and took the elevator up to the penthouse.

Being Tuesday morning, he was probably getting ready for work. Or maybe he'd already left. She should've thought to check the garage for his Porsche.

She rang the bell.

A moment later, Hudson opened the door, looking as tall, dark, and ruggedly handsome as ever. She thought of Merrell. She did have a thing for tall and dark.

Hudson didn't mask his surprise.

She flashed a winning smile. "Long time, no see." She glanced past him. "You alone?"

"I am."

She took in his boxers and tee. "You working from home today?"

"I am."

"I got some good news this morning." She untied the wrap on her dress and let it slide down her back. She wore her navy lingerie set, the one Hudson liked.

It was slight, but she heard him draw in a breath.

Inside, she smirked. "I want to celebrate."

He hesitated.

"Just this once. It's all I want."

～

Nora and Hudson lay in bed after a marathon of sex. With his eyes closed, Hudson's breaths came steady, but he wasn't sleeping. She knew his sleeping breaths, and these weren't it.

She stared at the vaulted ceiling, her eyes wide. She hated that sex with Hudson was so good.

"You didn't even ask what I was celebrating," she said.

"What are you celebrating?" he mumbled.

"It doesn't matter." She let out a dramatic sigh. "Did you at least hear the podcast?"

"What podcast?"

"Yesterday. Ferris Palmer's. I was his guest."

"Missed it. Sorry."

"Did you hear I won The Florida Humanitarian Award?"

"Yes."

"Did you hear I was named one of 'The 20 Most Charitable Women of the Year?'"

"Yes."

"Did you hear about my donation—"

"Yes, Nora. I know about it all. I know you started The Merrell Hodges Foundation around this time last year. I know you're quite the philanthropist now. I know you bought a jet and you've been to Italy. I know pretty much everything. Just because we don't speak and I don't go to your church doesn't mean I'm out of the loop. Cooper keeps me up to the date."

"Well, you could've called and congratulated me on any single one of those things. Heck, a text would have been appreciated."

He rubbed his eyes. "Is that why you're really here? So I'll be in awe of your accomplishments?"

"Actually, I was hoping for an apology. The last time we were alone you treated me like crap."

He became quiet, clearly not recalling what Nora referred to.

"Chicago?" she reminded him. "February of last year."

Finally, Hudson opened his eyes. He sat up. "Jesus Christ, are you for real? You threw yourself onto the floor like a bratty toddler. You said Merrell would die soon and we could get married. Shit, Nora. If anyone owes an apology it's you to me."

"You're a dick."

"Excuse me?"

Nora shifted on the mattress and shoved him so hard he rolled and fell out of bed.

He landed with a heavy thud and it took him a second to realize what had just happened. "Get out of my house."

Naked, she flew over the mattress and slapped him across the face.

Hudson shot to his feet. "Get the hell out of my house!"

Nora reared back for another slap. He grabbed her wrist and flung her to the side. Her ribs connected with the bedside table and she cried out. "I can't believe you just hit me!"

"Hit you?" He laughed.

Holding her side, she scrambled away from the table

and to her lingerie draped over a corner chair. Nora put the chair between them as she hastily dressed.

"You are crazy," he barked, reaching for his boxers on the floor.

"You touch me again and I'll scream so loud this whole place will hear."

"Go ahead!" he challenged.

Nora yanked her panties up her legs. "You told him, didn't you?"

"Told who, what?"

"Oh, don't act innocent." She snapped her bra on. "You told Merrell we were sleeping together. That's why he cut me out of the will."

"Hell, yeah, I told him." Hudson put his arms through a tee shirt. "He asked and I didn't lie."

Nora screamed.

Hudson marched over and yanked her from behind the chair. He dragged her across the penthouse, grabbing her purse, dress, and shoes as he went. She kicked and clawed and shrieked. He opened the door, threw her into the hall, and hurled her belongings over her head. They bounced off the opposite wall.

Then he slammed the door in her face, leaving her half-dressed in the exterior hallway.

Through the barrier he said, "I'm giving you exactly five seconds, then I'm calling the cops."

"Up yours!" she screamed.

"One."

Nora kicked the door. "You son of a bitch."

"Two."

She looked around for anything to break, but the damn hallway had nothing.

"Three."

"Fine!" she yelled.

"Four."

Nora finished dressing.

"Five!"

"I'm going!"

Through the door, she heard him dialing his phone. It came through loud over the speaker. "Palm Beach County Police Department, how can we assist you?"

"I said I'm going!" Nora shouted. She grabbed her shoes and purse before hitting the down arrow on the elevator.

It opened, and she stepped inside. She rode it down floor by floor to the garage. By the time the door opened there, she had finished dressing and moved on to snickering.

Men were so easy to manipulate. All she had to do was wear his favorite lingerie and she had him beyond ready.

She'd suspected Hudson told Merrell about the affair, but now she knew for sure.

Whatever, it didn't matter. She didn't need Merrell's stupid money. She had plenty of her own now.

She drove home, and the closer she got, the more she laughed. "One," she mimicked. "Two..."

Minutes later, she walked in her front door, still smiling. She found Elizabeth in her bedroom, doing homework at her desk. "What are you doing home from school?"

"Teacher workday."

"Men are stupid, Elizabeth. Remember that."

"O...kay."

"Let's have some mother-daughter time on the beach." She clapped her hands. "Meet me downstairs in ten minutes."

34

"It's pristine, isn't it?" Nora asked, taking Elizabeth's hand. "Do you know what that word means?"

"Pretty?"

"Yes, but more untouched I think." She pointed to the afternoon light dancing across the ocean to the horizon. "See here how the tide has come and gone. We're the first footsteps. It's lovely and unspoiled."

Her daughter paused to squish her toes in the wet sand and Nora smiled.

They walked a little further, enjoying the salty breeze and the grainy feel beneath their feet.

"Do you miss your father?" Nora asked after some time.

"Every day."

"I never really had a father. My mama married and divorced ten times before I was sixteen." Nora squeezed her hand. "I've never told anybody that."

"Not even Daddy?"

"Not even him." She watched the rise and fall of the surf as it smoothed the sand beneath them. "It was hard growing up with Mama. We were very poor. She kept remarrying, thinking that would help, but it never did." Nora looked down at her daughter. "If you let your past take over the present and mold the future, you'll never break the cycle."

She looked out over the ocean. "I thought I had it made with your daddy, but I lost it all. Now, I'm climbing back. I'm tough. There is nothing out there that will end me. I want you to be the same way. Nothing should ever stop you, not even me."

Elizabeth nodded.

They continued walking, hand in hand, and Nora's thoughts drifted. "When I was a little girl I wanted to be a dancer. A ballerina. I never had lessons, but I used to practice moves. I was good. Limber. I had great balance."

Nora let go of Elizabeth's hand and twirled away, demonstrating her moves. She motioned for her daughter to try and Elizabeth mimicked her whirls. Laughing, Nora took her hand again and they skipped along the sand.

A few seconds later they slowed to another walk.

"Girls have it hard in this world, Elizabeth. You have to do things boys don't just to survive. You have to be smart and never give up. You remember that, okay?"

"I will," Elizabeth said. "I'll remember."

Nora walked up the sand and sat down, pulling her daughter down beside her. They gazed out at the ocean. "This is how we used to be," Nora said. "We were bosom buddies. We used to play and dress alike. Do you remember? Then, something changed. You started liking your daddy more than me. It hurt my feelings, Elizabeth. I want us to be buddies again." She squeezed her hand. "Can we be buddies again?"

Elizabeth nodded.

"I still remember the first day I saw your daddy. He was

preaching. I wanted to do bad..." Nora's voice trailed off. She chuckled. "When you get older I'll tell you that part."

She put her arm around Elizabeth. "I never wanted a child. I was afraid, I think. But something changed the day I held you for the first time. I wanted you. I was glad to have you. You were perfect and all mine. I was going to be such a good mother. I would love you and not be afraid." Nora kissed the side of her daughter's head. "It's just you and me now. We'll never be alone. We'll always have each other. I'm yours and you're mine. I would give you anything. Would you give me anything?"

Elizabeth hugged her and Nora felt loved, wanted, and safe. "Yes," her daughter said. "I would give you anything."

"Are you happy to be with me, Elizabeth?"

Elizabeth gazed at her with an intensity that reminded Nora of herself, not Merrell.

"Are you?" she prompted.

"Yes, Mother, I'm happy."

Nora smiled. "I want you to love me. Do you?"

"I do."

Tears filled her eyes and she hugged Elizabeth tight. "Mothers and daughters have unconditional love. Do you know what the means?"

Elizabeth shook her head.

"It means we love each other no matter what. No matter what you say or do to me, I'll always love you. The same goes for the other way. No matter what I say or do to you, you'll always love me." She squeezed her tighter. "Remember that, daughter."

35

Christmas came as did the annual children's event hosted once again by The Merrell Hodges Foundation and covered by the Christian Television Network as well as local media.

Elizabeth turned ten.

At the first of the year, Nora stood alongside Ferris Palmer for the weekly broadcast. Each Sunday she'd watch the playback, pleased that she always received the camera time whether it was her time to speak or not.

Cooper and the board noticed.

Winter turned to spring. Ferris transitioned back to the junior pastor spot and Nora took center stage. The ratings soared. Every week she worked with Cooper on the sermons, and every week she put her own spin on it. Those spins were what made her popular, as were the continued very public donations to various children's charities on behalf of the foundation.

Spring transitioned to summer and the invitations came in. She spoke at conferences, gave lectures at universities, traveled abroad for tours, and sold out convention centers.

"The 20 Most Charitable Women of the Year" list came out again and Nora made #15, right under Angelina Jolie. Oprah still took #1.

Summer rolled into fall and with that came a book deal, magazine covers, and guest spots on TV. Though Cooper never said it, Nora knew she was more popular than Merrell had ever been. The foundation she started in his name thrived. Cooper offered time and again to find someone to run it, but Nora refused. At this point, she no longer needed that money; she simply loved knowing that she had pulled the whole thing off. The only other person who knew was Mama. But Nora—or rather the foundation—took such good financial care of Mama, she wouldn't mutter a word.

Fall moved into winter. Every Sunday she stood on that stage with Elizabeth and Raina in the front row. Was Nora living her best life? Sort of, but she still wanted more. She wanted her own talk show. Her own magazine. A product line. Several island homes. Nora didn't want to just beat out Oprah for that #1 spot, she wanted to *be* Oprah.

Nora wanted this year's Christmas children's event to be the biggest ever with national coverage and kids shipped in from all over. It was as she was meeting with Cooper to finalize the event that Nora received a phone call that her mama was dying.

Nora wasn't going to go say goodbye, but Cooper insisted. How would it look to your followers if you let your mother die alone?

Reluctantly, she agreed.

She boarded the jet to California.

Some moments in a person's life alter their world either for the better or the worst. Nora would look back on this moment and realize that saying goodbye to her mama was the worst decision of her life.

36

Nora sat beside her mama's bed in ICU, holding her hand. On her lap lay a sealed envelope.

"Your mother said to give this to you if you showed up," the nurse had said.

"And if I didn't show up?"

"She said to shred it."

With that, the nurse left them alone.

That was thirty minutes ago and all Nora had done was sit here and stare at her mama. It had been two months since they last talked. She had no idea Mama had come down with a cold that moved into pneumonia. Her lungs were full, her breathing shallow, and with a consciousness that came in and out, the doctors weren't confident she'd make it through the day.

Once upon a time, her mama had been beautiful, but now she lay swollen from medicine and gray from sickness. Mechanical ventilation prohibited her from speaking.

She stared at the bluish tint of her mama's lips, imagining the pink lipstick she always wore. No wonder Nora hated the color pink.

"I've often envisioned this moment," Nora mumbled. "I've thought about what I would say. What you would say. You may not think about the past, Mama, but I do. Do you even realize how horrible you were to me? I've spent my entire life despising you. Time heals all wounds? I'm not so sure about that. Now that I'm a mom I wonder a lot about your mother. We never talked about her. I bet she was mean to you. You didn't get the way you are all by yourself."

Her voice trailed off as did her thoughts. They rewound through the years, flashing from one memory to the next.

"Do you remember that time you lied to one of your husbands? Harold was his name. You took money from his wallet and told him I did it. He whipped me hard for that with his brown leather belt. You stood there and let him.

"Or what about that time you locked me in a closet for three days? You had just gotten divorced again. Jonas was his name. I loved Jonas. He was kind to me. I snuck out to see him. I missed him so much. You found out and lost it. Three days in the closet, Mama. I would have rather you beat me than lock me up like that."

Nora shook her head as more memories flooded in.

"I used to love school. Do you remember that one teacher, Mrs. Doughtery? She took a liking to me. She knew something was going on at home. She worked with me during the day. I quickly went from an F student to an A. But I still failed that year because you stopped letting me go to school. You told them I had strep. Then the measles. Then whatever else. Bottom line, you were jealous of my relationship with Mrs. Doughtery, weren't you? That was fifth grade. I had to repeat that year. You moved me to a different school so I wouldn't have Mrs. Doughtery again. All the kids knew that I had failed, though. They teased me. Yet, the following year when I really did get strep, you wouldn't let me stay home. You made me go to school. You had just married that Pentecostal preacher. Vern was his name. He convinced you to pray the strep away. My tonsils were covered in white puss. Yet every morning the two of you laid hands on me and prayed and then sent me to school. Eventually, the school nurse discovered my tonsils and called you. You acted surprised to hear the news. Like you didn't know I had a fever and a white throat. That's the only reason why you finally took me to the doctor. Months later, Vern left.

"Then came your marriage to Tony. I did not like him. I told you he hugged me too much. He would come into my room uninvited. He used to watch me get ready in the morning. He creeped me out. You told me I was exaggerating. I wasn't. I was fourteen then. I ended up reporting him. The cops came to our house. Tony packed up and left. You lost it. You called me a whore. I watched you cut a switch from a tree. I watched you march inside the house. I knew it was going to be bad. But I didn't care. Tony was gone. I told you I was ready for my punishment. That threw you off. You expected a good struggle, didn't you? But I stood there and you beat me, and beat me, and beat me with that tree branch."

Nora's breath shuttered in and out. Of all Mama's husbands, Tony was the worst. Later he'd ended up in prison for child molestation. When Nora told her mama, she'd simply shrugged and said, "I knew he was a bad one."

A few seconds went by, more memories came. Nora didn't put voice to them. There were too many—the same, but different. Then there were the good times, like the time they saw *Annie* at the drive-in theater. Or the time they strung popcorn for Christmas. Or when Mama made her a jean skirt.

But shouldn't there be more good than bad?

With another sigh, Nora glanced down to the sealed envelope in her lap. "I guess I do owe you a thank-you. You were in between husbands, prowling for a new one—or at least that's what I thought at the time. Looking back, you were prowling for me. I was seventeen. You bought me a new dress and made me go to a tent revival with you. You sat me in the front row. You wanted Merrell to see me. And he did. Meeting him changed my life. Not even you realized how much. You've always been jealous of that, haven't you? All those husbands and you never once snagged a rich one. I did, though, on my first go-around.

"I could've been such a different person, Mama. I'm smart. Thanks to Merrell I went to college. I didn't need him to succeed, though. You made me think I did. Because of you, I did all the wrong things to Merrell. If I'd had a different role model, I'd be a different person. I'd be a good person. But I've got an ugliness inside. I'm dishonest. I'm narcissistic. I'm sneaky. And it's all because of you. You didn't teach me how to be good. You showed me how to be bad."

Nora stopped talking. She studied their clasped hands. She pressed her manicured finger into the dry skin on her mama's wrist.

More memories railroaded her, and she closed her eyes.

The ventilator clicked.

A nurse came and went.

Nora breathed.

Eventually, she looked up, ready for the final goodbye, only to find Mama's eyes open and focused downward to Nora's lap and the sealed envelope.

Nora thought about tearing it up and throwing it in the garbage. Instead, she broke the seal.

Dear Nora,

If you're reading this it means you showed up for a final goodbye.

Good girl.

I'm sitting in my condo that you and Merrell bought me looking back on my life. I can honestly say, nothing about it makes me smile. I pretty much dreaded every single day.

I had a hard childhood. I was raised by a Bible-thumping preacher dad and mousy timid mom. As far back as I can remember I was either working on our small farm, helping Mom in the house, or sitting in church listening to Dad.

I hated every day. I couldn't wait to leave.

When I was sixteen I went to my very first town party. I got drunk and the boys passed me around. I not only lost my virginity that night but I also wound up pregnant with no clue which boy was the dad.

I hid the pregnancy from my parents and tried to give myself an abortion several times. But nothing worked and you stayed firm inside.

My parents thought I was getting fat. They were so stupid.

I had you one night in my twin bed right there in our little farmhouse. My scream woke my parents and they ran into my room as I was pushing you out.

Two days later they packed my belongings, gave me one hundred dollars, and told me never to come back.

I had you, one suitcase, and the hundred dollars. I hitchhiked my way from state to state, not sure what to do. People took pity on me and gave me money. Eventually, I settled in Tennessee. I took a job at Waffle House. I rented a tiny apartment. I figured God made you stay inside of me for a reason. I promised to try my best. But you weren't easy. You cried all the time.

When you were one, I tried to smother you.

When you were three, I pushed you down a flight of stairs.
When you were five, I fed you rat poison.
When you were seven, I left you on the side of the road.

Despite my best efforts, God kept bringing you back to me. I knew there had to be a reason. I renewed my relationship with Him then and the Bible. He used you to test me in so many ways. Most of those tests I failed. I am only human.

If I had to pick out a regret, it would be the husbands I married and divorced. I don't know what I was thinking. I was in a bad cycle of needing to be taken care of and none of them did it as I deserved.

In the end, there was a reason God kept bringing you back to me. Look at who you've become? Don't get a big head over that. That compliment is more about me than you. Clearly, I did something right since you turned out so successful.

If you expect this letter to end in love, you're sadly mistaken. I have never loved you, or anyone for that matter.

I will say thanks for the condo and for paying my bills all these years. I knew you'd be good for something.

See you on the other side,
Mama

Shaking, Nora stood up. She glared down at her mama, still with her eyes open and focused. "Hear this, Mama, my last words. I hate you. Rot in hell."

Then she walked from ICU and her mama died that night.

37

Leaning in, Nora scrutinized her morning face. She pulled at the skin. She smiled. She frowned. She turned side to side.

Was that a new spot on her face? From sun or age, she wasn't sure but, yeah, a new spot.

She squinted her bloodshot eyes. She pressed her fingertips into the splotchy skin on her cheeks. Maybe she needed a facial.

Or to stop drinking vodka.

She was looking more and more like her mama every day.

An image of Mama lying in ICU, bloated and gray, flashed through Nora's head and she flinched.

She put drops in her eyes, then strapped the cold compress over her face. With a sigh, she turned off the bathroom light and walked into the master bedroom.

She looked at the unmade bed and her mama's voice filtered in. *You think you're so good you don't have to make your bed?*

With gritted teeth, Nora marched over. She flung the

sheets and comforter into place and threw the pillows against the headboard.

She turned away, going next into the walk-in closet. The ghost of her mama stood there, cramming her clothes into a black garbage bag. *You don't deserve these new clothes that Jonas bought you.*

She yanked a thin robe off a hanger and tied it on. She marched from the master suite and came to a stop at an open door that led into what used to be the nursery. A white rocking chair occupied the corner and Nora froze. It wasn't the same rocking chair, but still...

Her mama had pushed her into one just like it. *You will sit there until I decide you get up.* Nora had been twelve and just started her period. Scared to tell, she hid it. But when Mama found out, she was furious. Nora had sat in that chair all day and night. She bled through her clothes.

With a breath in and forced back out, she shoved that memory away. It had been a week since her trip to California and this was what happened every single day. Nora was exhausted. She desperately wanted to purge Mama's voice from her head.

She heard the water go off in Elizabeth's bathroom. A door opened. It closed.

Nora walked the length of the hallway. She looked into Elizabeth's bathroom. A wet towel lay on the floor. A wide-tooth comb sat on the tub's corner. The shower curtain was pushed back. Dark hair gathered around the drain. An opened tube of toothpaste leaked out. Spots littered the mirror.

You better come out of wherever you're hiding and face the music, Nora. The longer you stay hidden, the worse it will be.

Her fists clenched. She stomped across the bathroom and flung open the adjoining door. Elizabeth stood in her underwear. Startled, she reached for a towel and quickly wrapped it around her.

The mask strapped to Nora's face slipped and she yanked it off and threw it at her daughter. Rage she had never felt before boiled in her veins.

"Your bathroom is a mess!" she screamed.

Gripping the towel wrapped around her, Elizabeth took a step back. Her legs came up against the bed. "I-I'm sorry."

"You're sorry?" Nora looked around for anything to throw and found a flip-flop nearby. She grabbed it and hurled it at her daughter.

Elizabeth ducked and fell across her bed.

Nora flew across the room to the corner where a pile of stuffed animals sat. She grabbed them all and flung them one by one at her daughter.

Still holding the towel around her, Elizabeth scrambled off the bed to cower in the room's corner. Fear filled her eyes and Nora didn't care. It fueled her.

She took wide strides across the room to stand over her. Elizabeth cringed even further away like she thought the wall would suck her in. Nora reached down and grabbed the towel. She ripped away, leaving her daughter trembling in her underwear.

"You've got nothing I haven't seen!" Nora wrapped her fingers around Elizabeth's wrist and dragged her away from the wall.

Elizabeth screamed, but there was no one in the house to hear. Raina had left to run errands.

Nora kept a tight hold as she searched the bedroom for a switch. Of course, there wasn't one, but she found a fairy wand. She snatched it up and beat her daughter with it.

"Stop!" Elizabeth cried. "Please, Mother. Stop!"

"Oh, it doesn't even hurt!" Nora yelled. "It's a fairy wand!"

She stopped the whipping but kept a tight grip on her daughter's wrist. Nora dragged her across the throw rug over to the bathroom door. "Raina is not your maid. She is *my* maid, not yours. You will learn how to clean up after yourself."

Shoving Elizabeth into the bathroom, Nora pointed at the hair in the tub. She ran her finger across the spotted mirror. She grabbed the toothpaste and squeezed it all over the counter. She picked up a wet towel and snapped it across her daughter's legs.

Elizabeth cried out.

Nora yanked open the linen closet. At the bottom sat a double-sided bucket with cleaning supplies. She pulled it out, grabbed the first item she saw, and squirted her daughter.

"Stop!" Elizabeth's hands came up. "Please, Mother. Stop! I'll clean the bathroom. I promise."

Flinging the spray bottle into the tub, Nora pointed a finger in her daughter's face. "Ask nicely."

"M-Mother may I clean the bathroom?"

"Yes, you may. And if you tell Raina about this, you will never see her again." Then she stormed out, slamming the door behind her. Her daughter's soft cries echoed out.

Nora knew she'd lost it. She knew she was being crazy. But she couldn't stop. When she reentered the master suite, she waited to hear more of her mama's words, but her brain was blessedly quiet.

38

A silver Christmas tree decorated with dark blue ornaments dominated the living room. It towered twelve feet in the corner with open packages piled beneath it. Nora and Elizabeth sat side by side on a white leather love seat with a reporter from Christian Television Network to the right and a cameraman behind him.

Cooper hovered in the corner. Beyond him and out on the terrace children played with gifts that had been opened. Santa Claus sat in the middle laughing and chatting with them.

Into the camera, the male reporter said, "Merry Christmas from the Hodges home. No holiday special would be complete without a sit down with Nora Hodges. Thank you, Nora, for chatting with us. It's been a fun and busy day around here."

"Indeed," Nora agreed. And if one more kid put his slimy finger on her, she'd scream.

"You lost your mother just a few weeks ago. My condolences. How are you doing?"

Nora kept her smile in check. "It's been a challenging time. Thank you for asking."

"It's very kind of you to open your home, as you do every year at this time."

"I'm happy to have everyone." She'd be happier with a double vodka.

"You lost your beloved husband two years ago now. Within a few months of that tragedy, you established the Merrell Hodges Foundation, which sponsors this event, and has allowed for sizable donations to children in need. You were presented with the prestigious Florida Humanitarian Award. You were twice named one of 'The 20 Most Charitable Women of the Year.' Earlier this year you stepped up, contributing once again to the weekly televised broadcast that first introduced you and Merrell to the world. You've sold out arenas with your motivational sermons. And the list goes on. Anything coming down the line you want to tease us with?"

Nora let out a good-natured laugh. "Oh, heavens. God has been good to me. There's no telling what might transpire next." Another trip to Italy might be nice. Or sex with a stranger. Or a giant doobie.

The reporter looked at Elizabeth. "You turn eleven today."

"Yes, sir," she responded brightly.

Nora had given her talking and acting points for this interview. She knew better than to mess this up.

"How do you like celebrating a birthday on the most famous holiday of the year?" he asked.

"My parents used to work hard to separate my birthday from Christmas. They wanted me to have my special day, but I like combining the two."

Two birds with one stone, Nora thought.

Elizabeth clasped her hands in her lap and smiled. "I love having everyone here!"

The reporter chuckled. "Your parents are known for their generosity with children in need. I spy opened packages under that tree. Are those yours?"

"They are, yes. I always pick two to keep and I donate the rest."

"Elizabeth, you are such a delightful young lady."

"Thank you." She smoothed the lines of her new emerald green dress, then crossed her legs, looking very much the prim little lady.

The reporter went back to Nora. "Tell me about your fondest holiday memory."

"That's an easy one." She looked over at Elizabeth. *You're going to hate that kid.* "The year this sweet gift came into our lives."

Her daughter gazed at her in perfect adoration. Nora's eyes twitched ever so slightly, silently telling Elizabeth not to overdo it.

"Did you get up early this morning, Elizabeth?" the reporter asked.

She giggled, and with flawless memorization of the lines said, "Yes, I drive my mother nuts. But she always makes homemade donuts on Christmas morning and I wake up so excited to eat one."

Raina made the donuts but whatever. "Very true. Last year she ran into my room at five in the morning to get me up." Gently, she tugged at the end of Elizabeth's French braid. "I would be disappointed if she didn't." If her daughter ever came in at five in the morning, the house better be on fire.

"After that, we went to church and then came back here

to get ready for everything." Elizabeth glanced over at the tree.

"Of the whole day, what's your favorite thing?" the reporter asked.

"The donuts, of course!"

He laughed and so did the cameraman. His deep chuckle drew Nora's interest. She hadn't really noticed him until this moment.

"What will you two do tonight?" The reporter smiled.

I wouldn't mind doing the cameraman, Nora thought. Instead, she said, "We'll help clean up after everyone leaves." Which better be soon. "But for us, Christmas is a time of reflection. It's about our Father's gift, the celebration of Jesus being born. We'll read several favorite verses. I'm happy to share the list for your viewers."

"That would be great. Thank you, Nora and Elizabeth, for once again inviting us into your home on Christmas Day."

Nora looked straight at the camera. Her voice came through warm and heartfelt as she delivered the last line. "Thank you and a very blessed day to you and yours."

When the camera light went out, Nora stood. She tugged on the hem of her red satin jacket, straightening it to a perfect line. She shook the reporter's hand. "Would you like a tour of the house by Elizabeth?"

"Yes!" His face lit up.

She looked at her daughter. "Why don't you start upstairs?"

With a nod, Elizabeth motioned for him to follow. As they started up the steps, Cooper thumbed over his shoulder toward the terrace. "I'll see how everyone is doing out there."

Nora waited until he was outside and Elizabeth was all the way upstairs before turning to the cameraman.

Tall, dark, and handsome, he was her type. She stepped forward. "How old are you?"

"Twenty-five. Why, how old are you?"

She laughed. She liked him. "Forty-six."

"You're old enough to be my mother." He gasped.

Playfully, she narrowed her eyes.

He leaned in. "My name is Vick."

"Well, hello, Vick." She shook his hand, pleased to find it warm and strong. "You got any plans tonight?"

"Nope."

"Want to come back later?"

"Depends. You really going to read Bible verses?"

"No, probably not."

"Then, yeah, I'll come back."

39

That night, Nora stood behind the terrace bar, smiling at Vick as he opened the sliding glass doors and stepped through. She'd left a note on the front door that said, *I'm on the terrace.*

Slowly, he walked toward her. "Where's the munchkin?" he asked.

"It's ten. She's in bed."

"And the maid?"

"She's spending Christmas with her sister." Nora held up the vodka. "This okay?"

He shrugged. "I'm more of a beer kind of guy."

As Nora poured herself vodka and him a beer, Vick wandered across the terrace. He came to a stop at the steps that led down to the beach.

"Quite the place you got," he said, staring out at the moonlit ocean.

She carried both glasses over to him. "I can't complain."

When you were one, I tried to smother you.

Nora paused. Vick glanced over, his eyebrows raised. "Something wrong?"

She shook her head, and with her best flirtatious smile, she handed him the beer. They toasted, then sipped as they studied each other over the rims.

When you were three, I pushed you down a flight of stairs.

Nora's jaw clenched.

This time his eyebrows came together. "You sure you're okay?"

"I'm fine." She took another sip.

When you were five, I fed you rat poison.

Nora turned away. She downed her vodka.

When you were seven, I left you on the side of the road.

Vick touched her arm. "We don't have to do this…"

She took a breath and pushed it out. Without looking at him, she said, "Vick, I need my mind to be blank. Do you mind if we skip the get-to-know-you foreplay and get right to it?"

"Lead the way."

She walked back across the terrace to a lounge chair. She didn't have to look to know Vick followed her. Wearing a low cut V-neck dress with a side slit, she sat and crossed her legs. The powder blue material opened wide to reveal her tanned and lean thigh.

I tried to give myself an abortion several times.

Vick's lips twitched into a charming smile as he approached. He wore gray slacks and a white coastal shirt perfectly unbuttoned to tease dark chest hair.

Nora held out a hand, inviting him to sit beside her.

I have never loved you.

He ignored her invitation as he put his beer on a side table and slid his hand hungrily along her exposed thigh. She loved that he took the initiative. Vick placed her empty glass beside his beer. Nora uncrossed her legs. She stretched out on the lounge chair, bringing her right leg up. The dress slid open to offer a peek of white lingerie edged with lace.

You're nothing but a whore.

She caressed her fingers over her bare knee and down along her inner thigh. Vick eyed her movement. He reached out a hand and she playfully tapped it away. While he continued watching, she moved her fingers from her inner thigh toward her panties. She opened her right leg further, teasing him with the sight. Slowly, she stroked herself, keeping her gaze on his sexy face as she brought herself to climax.

Vick couldn't take it. He came down on top of her, passionately kissing her. His hands gripped her panties and he yanked them down her legs. His mouth replaced her fingers. She rode another climax before pushing him onto his back. Together they worked his pants open and she pleasured him with her mouth.

He came loud, not caring if anyone heard. It turned her on even more, that and the fact his erection didn't go away.

He grabbed her around the waist and she straddled him, wet and ready. She rode him hard and this time they both climaxed loud.

A good solid minute ticked by. Nora's mind was blessedly blank.

She opened her eyes, about to climb off Vick, when she saw Elizabeth standing in the shadows, watching.

40

The next few days went by. Nora didn't say anything to Elizabeth. Elizabeth didn't say anything to Nora.

They both silently existed in the house.

Another Sunday came around. They went to church. Elizabeth sat in the front row. Nora did her weekly broadcast.

She began to wonder if she'd actually seen Elizabeth or only thought she did.

She got her answer the following evening around eleven at night. Nora left her bedroom and went downstairs for a late-night snack. She walked into the dark kitchen and saw Elizabeth on the terrace.

Vodka glass in hand, her daughter strolled around the pool. She stopped to sip and she coughed. She made a face and poured it out. Then she started walking again, stopping here and there to sip an imaginary drink and talk to an imaginary friend. She flipped her hair over her shoulder in a flirtatious move. She winked and giggled. She slid onto a lounge chair and crossed her legs, laughing and drinking more imaginary vodka. Dressed in a long sleeping tee, she laid back and opened her legs. She fingered herself as she imitated a loud orgasm.

Nora stood in the kitchen, watching. But she didn't go to Elizabeth. Instead, she went back upstairs and left her daughter "drinking and masturbating" on the terrace.

∼

THE NEXT MORNING, Nora got up before Elizabeth. She made blueberry smoothies and added a small scoop of peanut butter.

She had the whole day planned. Now, she just needed to execute it.

When her daughter walked into the kitchen not long after, Nora handed her the smoothie.

"I thought we might take a little road trip today. What do you think?" she asked, sipping her smoothie.

"Okay, I guess." Elizabeth drank a healthy amount. "When's Raina coming back?" She frowned down into the smoothie. "This taste funny."

"Raina will be back in a few days. She deserved the time off. She works hard for us." Nora turned away. "Drink that up. It's got lots of great things in it. Plenty of energy for the day."

Elizabeth took another big sip. Nora hummed as she watched the clock.

Her daughter moved over to the kitchen table.

Nora poured a cup of coffee. She took a drink. She cleaned the blender and her glass. She heard Elizabeth rasp. She took another sip of her coffee. She glanced again at the clock.

Another rasp filled the air.

One more bit of coffee and Nora finally turned to see Elizabeth clawing at her throat. Her lips swelled. Her skin turned blue. Her eyes bulged. She fell over.

Nora put her coffee down and dialed 911. While she waited for them to arrive, she cleaned Elizabeth's glass.

It was just peanut butter. Not like it was rat poison or anything.

∽

"SHE'LL BE OKAY," Elizabeth's pediatrician said.

Nora wrung her hands. "Oh, thank God. I wasn't sure. The EpiPen was upstairs. By the time I ran and got it...I just wasn't sure. The last time this happened she was five." Nora hugged the doctor. "Thank you so much for coming to the ER."

The pediatrician clasped her shoulder. "You're welcome. It's very scary. I know."

Nora sniffed and glanced over to the closed curtain where Elizabeth was now resting. "I'm really worried about her."

"What's going on?"

She led Elizabeth's doctor a few paces away. "I...I'm not sure this was an accident. About a week ago I found her drunk on vodka. I don't even know where she got the alcohol. I run a dry household. I got her sobered up. I tried to talk to her about it, but she wouldn't communicate. She's been very quiet and to herself. The times she does talk it's to an imaginary friend. Then this thing with the peanuts. She knows she's highly allergic and not allowed to have it. I don't keep it in my house. I don't know where she got it. That's only the beginning. There are other things. Like one time she scrubbed her mouth with soap so hard that she bled.

She lies about everything. She gets angry over the simplest things. She makes her dolls fight each other. I found her eating dog food another time. She's tried to run away from home." Nora looked down. "I don't know what to do. I haven't told anyone. It's all been since her dad passed. She's not coping." She pressed her fingers to her lips. "Do you think she purposefully gave herself peanut butter? Do you think she's a danger to herself?"

41

The pediatrician took detailed notes and made recommendations, one of which was what Nora already had planned. Within the hour she placed a call to the private girls' academy she'd already picked out. She talked with the director, pouring on the concerned mother's act as she gave the same details that she had relayed to Elizabeth's doctor.

"You understand this has to be kept private, especially given who I am," Nora said.

"Of course," the director agreed. "We're a year-round behavioral and academic program that is faith-based. Our beliefs align perfectly with yours. We've had six decades of success. Our residential home is specifically designed for girls who are struggling. They learn to leave the entitlement and emotional turmoil behind. They become peaceful and healthy young ladies with care and concern for others. We encourage communication as they come to understand their own feelings. We feature a first-class program that repairs behavioral issues brought on by trauma, like the loss of a parent."

Yeah, yeah, yeah. Nora read the website. She didn't need the spill. "I don't want her to have visitors. I think it's important she immerses herself into the program."

"Yes," the director said. "We typically don't allow visitors until the first thirty days have transpired. Even then, they would need to be approved by you."

"Perfect," Nora replied. "I know the application and admissions process typically takes longer. I appreciate you moving things through."

"Well, when I heard Nora Hodges was on the phone..." the director confessed. "I'm a bit of a fan."

Nora rolled her eyes. "We'll see you tomorrow after her pediatrician releases her."

She left Elizabeth at the hospital and went straight home to pack her daughter's things and load them in the trunk. Nora spent the night in the hospital, more to make sure no one interceded. The following morning, they released Elizabeth.

Now here they were in the car.

Giant palm trees lined the side of the road. Nora's Mercedes whizzed past them. Elizabeth sat in the back, looking frail from yesterday's events.

"Where are we going?" she quietly asked.

"It's called Care and Hope. You'll be staying for the rest of the school year. Your pediatrician feels this is best. I agree."

Her daughter cast a panicked look out the window. "I don't understand."

"This place comes highly recommended. You'll go to classes. There's even a playground you're allowed access to once you prove you're responsible enough. They have horses and art classes. Plus weekly church service. They'll teach you about your mood and conduct disorder. You'll learn about your anxiety. It's very private and exclusive. Very expensive."

A desperate beat went by. Elizabeth sat forward. "Like a private school?"

"Yes, but it's focused on your mental health. You haven't been acting normal. I saw you on the terrace drinking vodka and touching yourself. That's one of the many things they'll want to talk to you about."

Her daughter's face turned red. "Please don't do this. I promise not to be bad anymore. I'll do everything you say. I won't talk back. I'll help Raina. Whatever you want."

Nora slowed the Mercedes as she pulled under an archway. The sign affixed to the stucco column read:

Care and Hope
A Faith-Based Academy for Girls

The Mercedes pulled up to a circular drive where a tall gray-haired woman in a black pantsuit waited. Nora recognized her from the website. Dr. Wong, the director. With a kind face and perfect posture, she smiled as they parked.

Before Nora got out, she said, "You've been sad since Daddy died. You talk about that as much as you need and want to. Frankly, Elizabeth, I'm concerned. Why did you put peanut butter in your smoothie? You know you're allergic."

"I...I didn't."

"See there? You're lying. Just like you've lied about other things. Like that time you scrubbed your mouth with soap. You told your daddy that I did it. It was only after we talked that you finally admitted you lied. Then there's the time you tried to run away from home. Or what about when you threw that doll away that I gave you? You chose Uncle Hudson's gift over mine. Normal girls don't do things like that. Don't get me started on the defiance. You never do what I ask."

Tears filled Elizabeth's eyes. "Please don't make me go. Please. When will I see Raina again?"

"I'm glad you asked. I want you to remember how much you love Raina. How well you do here determines if she continues living with us. You be a good girl and remember that a good girl doesn't talk bad about her mother. Do you understand?"

"Please." Her bottom lip wobbled. "Please don't make me go here."

Nora got out first, nodding for Elizabeth to do the same.

With tears in her eyes, she slowly opened the door. Nora lifted her chin, silently telling Elizabeth to be brave.

Dr. Wong approached. "Mrs. Hodges, it's an honor to meet you in person."

With a gracious smile, Nora shook her offered hand. "It's so nice of you to greet us."

"We're delighted and privileged to accommodate you and Elizabeth."

Nora looked over to her daughter's pained expression. "Don't be nervous, sweetheart. Come here and meet Dr. Wong."

Slowly, she approached.

"You'll be very happy here, Elizabeth." Dr. Wong smiled. "You'll see."

"I won't." Elizabeth shook her head, looking again at Nora. "Please let me come home. I promise to be better."

Nora sighed.

Dr. Wong didn't seem fazed at all. She placed a comforting hand on Elizabeth's shoulder. "Everybody who comes here is nervous. It's natural. It takes a brave person to walk in that door. Are you brave, Elizabeth?"

With a shrug, she looked down at her tennis shoes.

A man dressed in khaki pants and a white polo came through the door. He wore a nametag, but Nora couldn't read it from where she stood.

"I'll get her bags," he said and Nora pressed the trunk release on the Mercedes.

Dr. Wong kept her attention on Elizabeth. "You'll find this to be a lovely place. You'll make friends. Soon you'll be calling home to tell your mom all about your fabulous day."

Elizabeth watched the man take her bags from the trunk, then walk them inside.

"There's the paperwork we need to be signed," Dr. Wong said.

"Will you email that to me? I want my lawyer to glance over it. I'll have it back first thing tomorrow."

"Certainly." Dr. Wong exchanged another handshake, then Nora hugged and kissed Elizabeth.

"Please," Elizabeth whispered, clinging to Nora.

She gripped her shoulders in a loving but firm hold as she looked her in the eyes. "Now, that's enough. You be a good girl and go with Dr. Wong. You're going to be just fine."

Tears dropped.

Nora got back into her Mercedes. She waved. Elizabeth stared at her car as she drove the long immaculate driveway back to the main road.

When she hit the highway, she cranked on the music.

At least she didn't leave her daughter on the side of the road.

42

Marathon sex with Vick, the cameraman. It was a good way to spend Nora's first days of freedom.

On Saturday morning, Raina returned. "Where's Elizabeth?" she asked. Not *How are you doing, Mrs. Hodges?* or *How was your holiday?*

"I've asked Cooper over," Nora said. "I'll explain when he gets here."

As if on cue, the doorbell rang and Raina answered.

Their mumbled voices filled the foyer. Nora had already made coffee and busied herself pouring cups for everyone.

Silently, Raina entered the kitchen with Cooper right behind her.

Nora slid them each a mug of coffee, but neither of them drank any.

She took a breath and let it out slowly. She focused on maintaining a concerned expression. "Last week we had the annual Christmas event. Cooper, you were here. It went well."

Carefully, he nodded.

"The following evening I came down to the kitchen for a snack and found Elizabeth on the terrace. She was passed out drunk."

Raina gasped.

Cooper made no expression.

"The next few days went by and I tried to talk to her about it, but she refused to have a conversation. We were at church on Sunday. Cooper, we saw you there."

Again, he carefully nodded.

"The next morning I came downstairs to find my private stash of peanut butter open on the counter. Elizabeth had eaten a huge spoonful and was barely breathing. I called nine-one-one. Her pediatrician met us at the ER. They talked in private. Bottom line, the pediatrician feels Elizabeth is a danger to herself."

"This doesn't sound like Elizabeth," Raina said.

"Where is she?" Cooper asked.

Nora took a sip of her coffee. "I know you're both upset. I am too."

"Where is she?" Cooper demanded.

Nora held a hand up. "She's at a place called Care and Hope. It's a faith-based school for girls who are having issues dealing with life."

"I want to see her," Raina said.

"I know. I do too. But the program is total immersion for the first thirty days. After that, she's allowed to have visitors."

Nora looked between the two of them. "I didn't want to alarm you two. Raina, you deserved your time off. I knew you'd come running. I handled it."

"I want to talk to her pediatrician," Cooper said.

"That's fine, but you know she's legally not allowed to

say anything." Nora took another sip of coffee. "People will wonder why she's not in church every Sunday."

"I'll handle that," Cooper quickly said. "Thirty days?"

"Yes, thirty days until her first visitor. However, the program does, at a minimum, require her to finish out the school year."

"It's six months until summer!" Raina nearly yelled.

Six months for Elizabeth to learn her lesson. By the time she returned, she'd kiss Nora's feet.

43

For thirty days, Nora felt like a new woman again. She came and went as she wanted. Raina stayed out of her way. She delivered a powerful sermon every Sunday. She enjoyed lots of sex with her new toy, Vick. Sex with Vick was almost as good as sex with Hudson.

More importantly, she didn't think once about Elizabeth.

At the one month mark, Cooper reminded her. "I want to go with you to see Elizabeth."

Nora replied, "I talked with the director and she said first visits are for family only. I'll go this first time. I'll ask about you and Raina. Don't worry."

Cooper did not like that response.

Nora drove an hour north to Care and Hope, and now she stood with Dr. Wong watching Elizabeth interact with other girls her age. She laughed. She played. At one point she walked over and took another girl's hand, encouraging her to join in.

"She looks happy," Nora grumbled.

Dr. Wong nodded her agreement. "In the short time Elizabeth's been here, she's made significant progress. She's quite popular. She's outgoing and friendly with a maturity level of someone years older. We work on a reward system here and she's already at the top. She has full privileges."

Nora frowned.

Her daughter hugged a girl smaller than her and then pulled back to say something. The smaller girl nodded and shrugged, smiling shyly. Another girl ran over and said something and Elizabeth gave her a playful punch in the shoulder.

Nora said, "What about the isolation room? Did you have to put Elizabeth in that?"

Dr. Wong gave Nora an odd look. "Not at all. That room is for extreme cases."

"She's a chameleon." Nora narrowed her eyes. "Don't let her fool you."

"I assure you, Mrs. Hodges. Nothing gets by us here. We're not easily fooled by any of the girls." Dr. Wong shifted, clasping her hands behind her back. "It's important that Elizabeth have family support, be it blood-related or not. She's asked about Raina, Uncle Cooper, and Uncle Hudson. As the legal guardian, you have the say. Does—"

"No. I do not give her permission to see anyone but me." Nora turned away. "I'd like to take her out to lunch. I'm assuming that's allowed?"

"Of course. Elizabeth!" Dr. Wong called out. With a wide smile, she glanced over her shoulder and her face froze when she saw Nora. "You're going to lunch with your Mom."

∽

AN HOUR later Nora and Elizabeth sat across from each other at a French restaurant. Nora's eyes roved the tables, hoping to catch someone taking a photo of her. Or someone staring in awe that Nora Hodges was here. But no one spared her a glance. If Merrell had been with her, more than one person would have noticed.

Elizabeth sat quiet and stiff in her chair like she was afraid to say or do anything.

"Oh, for God's sake," Nora snapped. "You look like death is hovering over your shoulders. Can't you smile? Any other little girl would be happy to be at a lunch date with their mother in a fancy French restaurant. But not you."

Forcing a smile, her daughter straightened her shoulders. She reached for a breadstick and broke it in half. She took a bite and chewed.

"Isn't that Nora Hodges?" someone quietly said from behind their table. With a smirk, Nora reached for her hot tea. This was more like it. "I heard Merrell left his entire fortune to the daughter."

With the tea halfway to her lips, Nora froze.

The waiter approached. "Are you ready to order?"

She put the tea back down. "Lamb chops with the Cognac Dijon sauce."

"And for you, miss?" The waiter smiled at Elizabeth.

Her daughter smiled back. "I don't know. Everything is in French. Whatever you think I'd like, I guess."

"Don't flirt, Elizabeth." Nora handed the waiter both of their menus with a polite smile. "Bring her lamb chops as well."

The waiter hesitated as if he wasn't sure about lamb chops for an eleven-year-old girl.

"Thank you," Nora said.

With a nod, the waiter walked off and Nora looked at Elizabeth's embarrassed face.

"I wasn't flirting," her daughter whispered.

"Whether you realize it or not, you were." Nora lifted the

fancy china cup and sipped the hot tea. "Now, tell me about Dr. Wong. Do you like her?"

Elizabeth brightened. "I do. I like everyone I've met."

"And to think you didn't want to go. Maybe this will show you that mother knows best." Nora arched a brow. "Hm?"

Her daughter nodded.

Placing the teacup back in the saucer, she said, "Sometimes I wish you were a baby again. You couldn't walk or talk. You depended on me for everything. You were a good baby. You never gave me problems. I thought I would come today and you would be this brand-new girl. But you're not. You're worse. I'm not sure being with Dr. Wong is the right decision."

Elizabeth's face fell.

"It's not exactly a cheap place. I'm not using your inheritance to pay for it. I'm using my own money." Nora waved her hand over the table. "You're only eleven and you don't understand, but this fancy meal? I'm paying for this out of my own money too. I wouldn't be here if it wasn't for you. You should be paying for this out of your inheritance."

Elizabeth swallowed. "Can't you take some of my money?"

"Yes," Nora sighed. "I suppose that will be all right. I started the Merrell Hodges Foundation and you haven't bothered to donate any money to it. After all, it is your father's legacy."

"I'm sorry." Elizabeth fiddled with her napkin. "How do I do that?"

"I'm glad you asked." Nora pulled paperwork from her purse. "This will let Uncle Cooper know that you want to donate money to your daddy's foundation." She held up a pen. "You just need to sign."

44

The next morning, Nora walked right into Cooper's office at church.

Abruptly, he stood. "I called you three times yesterday. How is Elizabeth? How was your visit? Is she okay?"

Nora waved that off. "Of course she's okay."

"When can I see her?"

She ignored the question as she sat across from his desk. "I took her out to lunch yesterday. People were gossiping in the restaurant about Merrell's will. That was supposed to be private. How did the information get out?"

"I don't know." Cooper took his seat. "It wasn't by me."

"Well, who all knows? You, Hudson, me, Raina..."

Vick.

Son of a bitch.

Nora held up a finger. "And don't say Raina is the leak. She knows better."

"I wouldn't say that about Raina. The only other person I can think of would be Hudson's secretary who did the paperwork, but I highly doubt she said anything. She's been with Hudson forever. She knows privacy laws."

"Well, somehow it's out," Nora snapped. "These kinds of things have ricochet effects. I'll lose the credibility I've built back up. My Sunday viewership will drop. Invitations to travel and speak will be rescinded. Donations to Merrell's foundation will stop."

"You're overreacting."

"Am I?" She looked away as her thoughts began to shift and swim. She could tell people it's what she wanted. In Merrell's last days, she asked him to change the will... Yes, that would work. She'd look like a saint for thinking of their daughter.

"Elizabeth, when can I see her?" Cooper asked again.

"Soon." She reached in her purse and brought out the paper Elizabeth signed. "She told me at lunch she wants to donate a monthly amount of her inheritance to Merrell's foundation."

Nora laid the signed document on Cooper's desk.

He picked it up, quickly perused it, and laid it right back down. "As the person who controls Elizabeth's trust, I can't approve this until I do a thorough audit of the foundation."

"That's not going to happen."

Cooper nodded to the paper. "Then neither is that. Now, I'll repeat, when can I see Elizabeth? And I'm going to need a better response than 'soon.'"

Nora considered negotiating. *Approve the document and you can see Elizabeth as soon as today.* Instead, she said, "I'm not sure. She's fragile. She's making progress but Dr. Wong feels it'll take time before she's ready for non-family visitors."

This, of course, was a complete lie.

Cooper didn't respond. He simply studied her.

Fine, he could study her all he wanted. She had the upper hand.

"What's it going to take?" he finally asked.

"For you to sign that." She crossed her legs and waited.

"Okay, let's negotiate. I'm aware you're paying for Care and Hope out of your own money. I'm also aware it's not cheap. Instead of signing that paper, I'll pay for Elizabeth's tuition out of her trust. In exchange, you will put me and Raina on the visitation list today."

Seeing as how Nora was already paying the tuition from Merrell's foundation, this accomplished the same thing. Either way, it wasn't coming out of her budget. "Deal."

She took the paper off his desk and stood.

"Your personal life is your business," Cooper said, "but might I suggest you don't have your young man coming in and out of your house in such a visible way."

"What are you talking about?"

"You're worried about the gossip surrounding Merrell's will? You should be more worried about the gossip surrounding the man you're having an affair with. You're old enough to be his mother. You're not Demi Moore. You are a televangelist. People expect you to act in a certain way."

Nora narrowed her eyes. "How do you know about that?"

"You have neighbors. It's not like they don't see the comings and goings. A couple of your neighbors even go to church here."

Nora didn't have a response.

"We both know how chatty you get when you've been drinking. Perhaps you told your young man about Merrell's will and he told others." Cooper sat forward in his chair. "You are your own worst enemy, Nora. You need to watch out. Your decisions will catch up to you. Be careful."

∽

SEX WITH VICK WAS PHENOMENAL, but not so outstanding that Nora would risk her career.

She broke up with him that afternoon.

One week later he posted a video of them having sex.

Within twenty-four hours, it had gone viral.

45

Give it to me rough.
Harder.
Harder!

If there was a cliché thing to say during sex, Nora had said it.

She was made into GIFs and memes.

SNL did a skit.

Night show hosts joked about her.

Morning talk shows discussed it.

She lost all invitations to speak.

She was forced to hand the Sunday broadcast back to Ferris Palmer.

The joke of the decade. That's what Nora became.

Instead of "The 20 Most Charitable Women of the Year," she'd hit the number one spot of the "Top 20 Most Embarrassing Moments."

She could hear her mama's voice. *Oh, how the mighty have fallen.*

Nora couldn't take it. She packed a bag, left the country,

and checked into a private resort in Greece. Eventually, things had to blow over, right?

Cooper called. So did Dr. Wong. Raina, too, and Elizabeth. Nora deleted every message. She was embarrassed and humiliated. If she could fall off the earth, she would.

Instead, she fell into a bottle of vodka.

It was on a Sunday morning in June when Nora realized she had blown through millions of dollars and couldn't pay her latest resort bill.

Left with no choice, she returned home.

But nothing had blown over.

∼

RAINA WALKED in the front door with Elizabeth, her school suitcases in tow.

Six months ago Nora had packed those suitcases. Six months ago she had ruled the world. Six months ago her face hadn't been plastered over every screen in America and beyond.

From her spot in the living room, she stood.

Suitcase in hand, Elizabeth paused. Her gaze met Nora's. The last time they saw or spoke to each other was the day Nora went to visit her at Care and Hope and took her out to lunch.

Her daughter didn't say hi.

Neither did Raina.

"Hello," Nora greeted them. "Long time, no see."

"M-Mrs. Hodges." Raina shook her head. "Did we know you were coming? Did I miss a message?"

"I thought I'd surprise you." Nora threw her arms up. "Surprise!"

Without a word, Elizabeth left her suitcases in the foyer and walked into the kitchen.

Raina tried for a smile. "I made sugar cookies. I know they're not your favorite. We have other things."

With a nod, Nora trailed behind her.

In the kitchen, Elizabeth stood quietly eating a cookie from a platter in the center of the island.

"I take it you're home for summer break," Nora hesitantly said.

Her daughter didn't answer. She didn't even make eye contact.

Raina began folding cloth napkins. "Yes, summer break."

"That's nice." Even though Nora didn't like sugar cookies, she still picked one up. "School has been good?"

Elizabeth swallowed her bite, still not looking at Nora.

Raina cleared her throat. "School has been very good. Elizabeth loves Care and Hope. Dr. Wong has recommended she be a mentor-in-training next—"

"Where have you been?" Elizabeth demanded, finally making eye contact.

Unexpected tears pushed at the back of Nora's eyes. "Greece," she whispered.

"Greece?" Elizabeth huffed an unamused laugh. "You could've called. Or a text even."

Nora didn't want them to, but the tears were too hot to contain. They shoved their way free. She bowed her head. She couldn't believe she was crying. "I'm sorry."

Silence fell in the kitchen.

"I was...*am* the most embarrassed I've been in my entire life." Her eyes closed. "I'm sorry I'm your mother," she murmured and the words rooted true and deep into her core, leaving her raw and exposed.

No one said a word.

A solid moment ticked by.

Her daughter moved then, closing the short distance, surprising her with a warm and firm hug.

Nora accepted the hug, holding tight. "I don't know what I'm going to do. I'm so scared, Elizabeth. Everything I worked hard to build after Merrell died is gone. My reputation is ruined. I can't show my face anywhere. Soon you'll be grown and gone. I won't have any place to live. Merrell left you everything." More tears came, gradually transitioning into a full-on sob. Nora couldn't remember ever having cried so hard in her life. She felt desperate and vulnerable. She needed her daughter. Elizabeth was all she had. "I'm so alone."

"You're not alone. I'm here. Raina's here."

"I'll give you two a minute," Raina quietly said and left the kitchen.

Nora held tight. "You're all I have now. I promise I won't embarrass you anymore."

"It's okay." Elizabeth rubbed her back. "You're going to be okay."

Relief moved through her and Nora sagged into her daughter's arms. She almost didn't recognize this mature girl. Dr. Wong had taught her how to be compassionate. Nora made a good decision taking her to the girls academy.

She hoped everyone realized that.

"Are you staying then or going to some new place to hide out?"

Nora pulled back and looked into her daughter's smiling eyes. "If you're not embarrassed by me, I guess I'm not either."

46

Throughout June, Nora came to depend on Elizabeth.

Her daughter made sure she ate.

She made sure she didn't drink too much vodka.

She reminded her she was allowed one cigarette per day.

She brought her inside when she passed out on the terrace.

On the nights Nora couldn't sleep, Elizabeth stroked her hair and massaged her back.

And when Nora did drink too much vodka, she nursed her through the hangover.

Best of all, she helped Nora hide it all from Raina.

Elizabeth had turned into the daughter Nora always wanted.

She couldn't imagine what her days would be like when she went back to school.

On a Friday night in late June, Elizabeth attended a slumber party, Raina spent the night with her sister, and Nora was left alone.

One vodka turned to two. Three turned to four. Five to six...

Nora sat on her bedroom floor with her back propped against a wall. Through blurry eyes, she watched her daughter empty her ashtray, pick up food wrappers, and put her room back in order.

Wasn't she supposed to be at a slumber party? What time was it?

Nora worked her swollen tongue around her mouth. She needed water.

Elizabeth hurried from her room and ran downstairs. Nora was just about to black out when her daughter was suddenly in front of her.

Nora smiled. "What time is it?"

"Morning." Elizabeth wrapped a cool rag around Nora's neck. "Raina will be home soon. We have to hurry." Elizabeth patted her cheek. "Wake up."

Nora didn't realize her eyes had closed. She forced them open. Her daughter gave her two ibuprofen, one vitamin B_{12}, and a cup of coconut water.

The ultimate hangover cure.

Elizabeth tipped the cup. "Drink all of it."

Nora's eyes closed. They opened. Her hazy gaze roamed over the bedroom. She looked down at her strapless red gown. Who put this on her? She patted it. "Pretty."

"I need to get you in bed. Can you stand?"

"If you ask nicely," Nora murmured.

Elizabeth sighed. "Mother, may I put you to bed?"

"Yes, you may."

Elizabeth hovered as Nora crawled across the wood floor and climbed up and into bed.

Her eyes were already closed as she smooshed her face

into the pillow. A comforter magically wrapped around her, and her body relaxed as sleep moved in.

Elizabeth reached under the comforter and took her shoes off. She repositioned Nora's head so she wouldn't get a kink in her neck. She stroked her hair.

What a good daughter. It was Nora's last thought before she drifted off.

47

On July 4, Nora wandered out onto the terrace. She found Raina sitting on the steps that led down to the beach.

Quietly, Raina took in the dark ocean and moonlit sky. In the distance, fireworks popped. Nora checked her phone. 8:30 p.m.

She sipped her vodka. "Where's Elizabeth?"

Raina pointed off to the left. "The Fischers are having a party. Their grandson is Elizabeth's age. He invited her to watch fireworks."

The Fischers lived four houses down. They owned dry cleaning businesses throughout Florida, Georgia, and soon the Carolinas. They hadn't invited Nora to this party.

Then again, no one knew she was hiding out at home.

She stepped down past Raina onto the beach. "Think I'll go for a walk." It was dark out. No one would notice her.

Nora kicked her flip-flops to the side and carrying her vodka, she trailed the sand to the ocean. She turned left and took her time, letting the salty water wash over her toes and up to her ankles.

She passed the first house on the left, smiling at its tasteful holiday decorations. The Laurents lived there. A couple, one a surgeon and the other a partner in a law firm. They had no children but two rescue dogs. The mutts annoyed Nora, always yapping and running the beach.

The second house stood dark and quiet. The Baileys lived there and were gone for the holidays. They owned a medical supply company and had a house in Colorado where they spent most of the winter skiing. Nora used to be friends with the wife, but they hadn't talked since before her sex video hit the waves.

The third house was currently under construction. The woman who bought the previous home tore it down and was rebuilding. Nora didn't know her name but she'd heard that the woman worked in finance.

She took the last sip of her vodka, now down to the ice and lime. She approached the fourth house where the Fischers lived. Like most of the homes on the beach, they had a terrace. Tonight people packed it, all dressed in Fourth of July themed clothes. Soft lights illuminated the interior and exterior. Lively music flowed through the air. Some partygoers had trickled out onto the sand to sit on blankets or in beach chairs.

That's where Nora found Elizabeth.

She sat on a red, white, and blue blanket next to a boy. He said something and she smiled. She said something and he laughed. He pointed to a sailboat in the ocean and Elizabeth leaned in to look. He pressed a kiss to her cheek, surprising her. She smiled, a little hesitant, and then her smile got bigger. He whispered something in her ear and she shyly glanced down as he linked fingers with her to hold her hand.

Nora saw red.

Gripping the glass she charged up the beach to where they sat. Simultaneously, they leaned in to kiss each other on the lips and Nora tossed the ice and lime over their heads. They jerked apart.

Her voice came out viciously. "Get up. Now. Both of you."

48

In the Fischers' home office, Nora paced back and forth in front of the older couple. Mr. Fischer sat behind a desk and Mrs. Fischer stood at the closed door. Both children sat at opposite ends of a leather couch.

Nora stopped pacing. She glared at Elizabeth. "I'm ashamed of you. You know better."

Her daughter didn't look at her.

Nora spun on Mrs. Fischer. "How could you let this happen? I allowed my daughter to come to your party and I find her making out with your grandson!"

"Mrs. Hodges, I understand you're upset, but please lower your voice." Mrs. Fischer nodded to the closed office door. "We have a house full of guests."

"We are Christians. I have raised a good girl. A proper young lady. Your grandson should be disciplined! Elizabeth would have never been doing all of that without him pressuring her."

Mr. Fischer cleared his throat and Nora turned her ire on him. He said, "They were holding hands. They're almost twelve. It was innocent."

"And they kissed! You didn't see what I saw." Nora jabbed her finger at the grandson. "He needs to be dealt with. If I hadn't interrupted when I did, who knows how far things would have gone!"

Mr. Fischer's voice came back strong. "My grandson is being raised right. He knows not to touch a girl unless he's given permission. He knows that 'no' means 'no.' I assure you, if you saw them kissing, then your daughter told him 'yes.'"

Nora's fingers curled into fists. She turned on Elizabeth. "We're leaving. Now."

Elizabeth finally looked up. Embarrassment flushed her cheeks and humiliated tears filled her eyes. Good, she should be mortified.

Mrs. Fischer stepped away from the door. "Mrs. Hodges, please, it truly was innocent. I think you're overreacting."

"And I think you're underreacting." She crossed the office to the couch and yanked Elizabeth up by the wrist. She pushed her to the door.

Mrs. Fischer hesitated, exchanging looks with her husband. Then with a sigh, she opened the door and stepped to the side. Nora shoved her daughter through.

She gripped Elizabeth's wrist as she charged through the house, across the terrace, and down to the beach back to their home.

"Oh my God, is that her? Is that Nora Hodges?" she heard.

With the vodka glass still in her hand, she snarled down into the empty tumbler. She could use a shot, or two, right now.

She threw the glass into the ocean. "I should have known you'd sneak off to make out with some boy. You are your mother's daughter." She lurched forward, cutting up the sand toward their terrace. "I don't want any more trouble from you tonight."

Raina still sat on the steps and she got to her feet when she saw them. Nora released her daughter. Raina looked between them before settling her attention on Elizabeth. "Did you have fun?"

"I caught her making out with a boy," Nora snapped.

Silence.

Raina looked puzzled.

"That's a lie," Elizabeth spoke.

Nora gasped. She spun around. "Inside. Now." She strode up the steps, across the terrace, and into their home. Elizabeth followed closely behind.

Downstairs their house had an open floor plan, but Nora wanted somewhere with a door to close. She headed straight up to the master suite. As soon as Elizabeth stepped inside, Nora slammed the door and whirled on her daughter.

For the first time, she saw fury on her daughter's face. It brought her to a pause. So much of a pause that Elizabeth finally demanded, "Well?"

"Why do you defy me?" Nora took a step forward.

"Why do you lie?"

Nora slapped her across the face. But Elizabeth didn't dodge or cower or even blink. She stood glaring back in a confrontational stance that unbalanced Nora. For the first time, she realized how tall her daughter had grown. They stood eye level now.

Enraged with Elizabeth's new poise, Nora slapped her again, harder. Even though her cheek flamed red, her daughter still didn't respond.

"You want me to hit you, don't you? Did Dr. Wong teach you this rebelliousness?"

"Dr. Wong taught me confidence."

Nora screamed.

Raina opened the door and Nora whirled on her. "Get out!"

Raina didn't move.

Nora got in her face. "If you want to keep your job, you will close this door and leave us be."

"I've got this," Elizabeth said.

"Are you sure?" asked Raina.

"She's *my* daughter!" Nora shouted, shoving the door closed and locking it.

"Why did you have me?" Elizabeth calmly asked.

"What?"

"You heard me."

"B-because your father and I wanted a baby."

"That's not true. Daddy wanted a baby. That's the truth."

Nora paced. "I don't know what to do with you. I don't know what to say to you." She threw her hands up. "I simply don't know." She frowned. "The truth is, I didn't want you. You're right. I did it for Merrell. Maybe even I did it because it's what everyone expected. A loving Christian couple and their child. I think I did it too to financially cement myself into Hodges Ministry." She huffed a laugh. "A lot of good that did me."

"And the truth comes out."

Nora's head snapped up. "Why do I even bother with you? You give everyone respect but me. I'm entitled to be honored and you never honor me. Never."

"Honor and respect go both ways, *Mother*."

Nora's body recoiled. She spun into the walk-in closet and came out with a thin leather belt. She lunged at Elizabeth, flicking it through the air. It connected with her daughter's bare legs. Elizabeth leaped onto the bed and

Nora followed her. The belt whipped across her neck. Elizabeth cried out and fell backward onto the bedside table. A lamp tumbled to the floor and Elizabeth followed.

Screaming, Nora flew from the bed onto the floor. She cracked the belt across her daughter's stomach. Elizabeth twisted out from under her and scrambled to her feet, but Nora grabbed her ankle and yanked her back. Elizabeth went down hard, her head bouncing off the wood floor. She stopped moving for a second and Nora whipped the belt along her back. Elizabeth flipped over and kicked out. Her foot connected with Nora's pelvis and she cried out.

The locked door rattled. Raina shouted, "I'm calling the police if you don't let me in!"

"You ungrateful brat!" Nora came at Elizabeth, flicking the belt through the air. Elizabeth's arms went up as she defended herself. The belt connected across both forearms, leaving a satisfying streak.

They moved across the bedroom as Elizabeth edged toward the door and Nora followed. Her daughter flipped the lock just as the belt cracked across her shoulder blades. The door flew open and Raina rushed in as Elizabeth pushed past her to get free.

Nora's arm came back, ready for another whipping when Raina stepped forward. "Stop this. Now!"

But Nora couldn't stop. She shoved Raina and Raina punched her once in the face. Sharp pain exploded under her eye and Nora stumbled back. Her spine connected with the wall and she slid down to her butt. Her body began to shake, with rage or hysteria, she couldn't be sure. But she released the belt and sobbed loudly.

What had she done?

49

Nora woke with a new resolve. She'd be better. Elizabeth would be better. They both needed to reconnect with God. This was what happened when you stopped praying, and Nora hadn't prayed with her daughter in nearly six months.

She found two stiff-backed chairs and placed them in opposite corners of the home office. Nora took one and put Elizabeth in the other.

Her daughter sat in a trance-like state as she stared dully at Nora.

Her mama did this with her when she was around Elizabeth's age. At the time Nora was so angry she couldn't see through her rage to the other side. But by the end of the day, they had turned a corner. They had forgiven each other.

Until they didn't.

But it would be different with her own daughter. The forgiveness would last.

Placing her hands on top of a Bible in her lap, Nora straightened her shoulders. "God has brought us to this moment so that we can see the error of our ways. We've sinned. We've transgressed against The Commandments. But we shall find forgiveness and be cleansed. Those who seek shall receive. Let's pray together for our repentance and that the Lord will grace us with comfort, wisdom, and guidance."

She slid from the chair to kneel. With stiff movements, Elizabeth did the same.

"Repeat after me." Nora bowed her head. "Dear loving Lord, I can hardly even bring myself into your presence when I think of what I've done."

Elizabeth robotically repeated it.

Nora continued, "I hurt myself and others. I have gone against you. I feel so wretched. It's hard to pray now."

She paused, waited on Elizabeth.

"Will you forgive me?" Nora asked. "Is it possible? Let me know, oh Lord, that it's not about me or my behavior but it's about your Son taking it all to redeem and purify me."

Again, she paused and her daughter spoke the lines.

"This is his work alone. This is why he came. Oh, dear Lord, let it pierce my heart and let my heart be changed." Nora's fingers pressed into the Bible. "Please forgive me."

Elizabeth's mumbled recitation filled the air.

"Please have mercy," Nora begged. "Pour out the blood of Christ over me. Cleanse me, Jesus, with your sweet love. In your holy name. Amen."

Peace filled her heart and she smiled as she listened to her daughter.

When Nora opened her eyes, light streamed in from the window. God was looking down on them. He approved.

Nora took her chair again, motioning for Elizabeth to do the same. They sat quietly on the stiff wood, looking at each other.

Hours went by, interrupted only by Raina checking on them.

Eventually, the sun set.

Nora was about to permit Elizabeth to get up when two men entered the office.

Cooper and Hudson.

50

Nora smiled big. "Cooper! Hudson!"

Neither man returned the smile. Cooper looked right at the bruise under Nora's eye where Raina had punched her.

Hudson walked over to Elizabeth. "Come on, sweetheart."

No expression crossed her face as she stood. Hudson put a gentle hand on her shoulder and led her from the office. Raina stood just outside in the hall. Elizabeth walked right into her arms.

Nora got to her feet, taking a second to shake her numb legs out. She waved them into the office. "Come in! Come in! Would you two like something to drink? Raina, get them a beverage."

Raina said nothing. She simply led Elizabeth away.

Cooper held up a hand. "This will be brief." He handed her a brochure. "I have chosen a rehab facility that you will immediately go to. I checked and they do accept partial insurance. Your monthly allowance will make up the rest. We are taking Elizabeth and Raina from this home until you are gone. You will no longer threaten Raina's job or immigration status. You will have no access to Elizabeth until you've completed ninety days of rehab. After that, you will not be allowed to see or talk to her unless one of us is present. If you choose not to go to rehab, I will contact the IRS about The Merrell Hodges Foundation. The only reason why I'm offering you this generous decision is that we don't want Elizabeth to see her mother dead and/or go to prison. Do you understand everything I just said?"

Nora kept her smile in check. "But Elizabeth and I are fine. Ask her. We prayed together all day." She looked from Hudson to Cooper, back to Hudson. "I don't know what you've heard. If Raina—"

"Stop it, Nora," Hudson snapped. "Raina keeps your secrets. She loves Elizabeth and she will do anything to stay here and protect her. And for whatever reason, that girl loves you too. Once upon a time, you were able to fool people, but you've lost it. The whole world knows who you are. Your little stunt last night at the Fourth of July party? Someone filmed it. It's all over social media."

Nora's smile fell away. "I know I've made mistakes, but—"

"Stop speaking, Nora," Cooper spoke. "We've told you how it's going to be." Next, he handed her a folder. "This document gives me co-custody of Elizabeth. You will sign this right now." He clicked a pen and handed it to her.

"This isn't what I want." Nora frowned. "I want her here with me. Like I said, we prayed—"

Hudson stepped forward. "This is no longer up for discussion. I will stretch my legal fingers across all of Florida and beyond if need be. You will comply or you will suffer my wrath."

Putting her palms together, she brought her fingers to

her lips. "This is my penance, isn't it? This is what God wants."

"Whatever you have to tell yourself," Cooper said, nodding to the custody paperwork.

51

The next day Nora entered rehab. Over the weeks that followed, she threw every bit of energy into the inpatient program. She passed each day eating and sleeping, attending AA meetings and workshops, and learning yoga and meditation. She got a sponsor and started working the steps.

Step One: She admitted she was powerless over vodka.

Step Two: She believed a higher power could restore her sanity.

Step Three: She opened her locked soul.

"I have a new outlook on life."

"The future is endless now."

"I've been given the stepping stones for recovery."

"I've accepted my flaws and will work on gaining trust from those I love."

These are all things she said and meant. *Just tell them what they want to hear*, her mama would have said. But Nora truly felt them. For the first time in her life, she was honest with herself. She stopped blaming her mama and took responsibility.

She vowed to no longer be the villain in her own story.

Step Four: She made a moral inventory.

Step Five: She admitted to her sponsor all of her wrongdoings.

Step Six: She recognized her character defects.

At the ninety-day mark, Cooper came to visit. "You look well."

"Thank you. I feel great. I'm ready to move into the aftercare stage where I'll be adjusting to life at home without relapsing. I'll be going to meetings, volunteering, and anything else to keep my mind focused on sober living."

Cooper offered a genuine smile. "I'm glad to hear. You are welcome to return to Merrell's home. Know that Raina will be giving me daily reports."

"When can I see Elizabeth?"

"She comes home from school this weekend. Raina will be there the whole time."

∼

OCTOBER MOVED INTO NOVEMBER. Nora talked with her sponsor daily. She focused on living a clean life.

Step Seven: She humbly asked God to remove her shortcomings.

Step Eight: She made a list of all those she had harmed.

That list overwhelmed Nora, and her sponsor suggested she make amends in small chunks.

The first chunk came in December when she hosted a small twelfth birthday celebration for Elizabeth. Cooper attended and so did Hudson and Raina. In front of them all, she completed Step Nine by making amends. Of the four of them, her daughter was the only one who responded favorably. The other three didn't say a word. Her sponsor told her to expect that. Still, it hurt.

The New Year turned over. Nora said goodbye to the old and welcomed in the new. Her relationship with Elizabeth slowly continued to heal.

Step Ten: She took a personal inventory every night, pleased at how well she was doing.

January transitioned to February. She began attending a small Bible study made up of men and women she'd met in AA. She worked on Step Eleven where she improved her contact with God.

In March she had officially been sober nine months and reached Step Twelve of spiritual awakening. She also turned forty-eight. Her sponsor told her not to go, but Nora felt confident. She treated herself to a long weekend in Vegas. She'd always wanted to see a real showgirls show, and she needed to prove to herself she could resist the temptations that a place like Vegas offered.

That's where she met Buford Steele.

Buford Steele was an eighty-two-year-old man who owned several casino boats throughout the south plus held shares in a couple of casinos in Vegas. He stood the same height as her with a bald head, thick black glasses, paunch belly, and flabby jowls. He saw her sitting alone at the show and asked to join. Nora almost said no until she saw the giant diamond ring on his pinky and the thick gold-linked necklace nestled in bushy gray chest hair. She smiled, he sat, and he bought her dinner.

He oozed money.

It stirred something dormant inside of her.

"I must admit," he'd said after the show, "I know who you are. I used to watch Merrell every Sunday on his weekly broadcast. I'd see you in that front row and just stare. I also went on to watch you when you took over the stage. I've always had quite the crush on you."

Nora wasn't sure if he knew how bad her reputation had become—surely, he had to—but she went with it, naturally flirting and turning on the Christian, good-girl charm that came second nature to her.

They talked for hours. He seemed clueless. Nora felt more like her old self—charming, beloved, and powerful—than she had in over a year. Like a recognizable, yet nasty little demon had been clawing and picking and was ready to be let free again.

That was a Saturday and by Sunday they stood in front of a minister who was dressed like Elvis. Nora said her vows. She married for the second time and like with Merrell, it was for the money.

Afterward, Buford reserved a section at Top of the World and now here they stood side by side with twenty or so of his Vegas friends and colleagues.

A champagne cork popped. Bubbles fizzed. Glasses were filled. Toasts came.

"To Buford and Nora!"

"A long and happy life!"

"Cheers!"

"Congratulations!"

Smiling, Nora and Buford clinked glasses. She took a delicate sip. Thankfully, she didn't like champagne and she had no problem putting the glass down. She exchanged a quick kiss with him, trying not to wince at his wet lips. More salutations came. Nora smiled at each. Beyond the restaurant windows, the night settled in. The darkness outside reflected their image. It showed Nora dressed in a gaudy pink business suit and Buford in a flashy purple one. It was what he wanted for a Vegas wedding.

Nora hated pink.

But she loved the extravagant diamond ring on her finger. She loved the expensive restaurant. She loved that he planned to whisk her away to the Maldives for their honeymoon. She loved he had vehicles and homes and a yacht. She loved that he had money and wasn't afraid to spend it.

And if she was being honest and allowing that nasty demon full reign, she also loved that Buford was eighty-two. That meant, at most, she'd have to put up with his wet lips for ten years. They hadn't consummated anything yet, but Nora hoped he didn't take Viagra. If he did, she'd have to figure out how to switch the pills out. She could do a couple of old man erections, but that was about it.

Phones came out. People took photos.

Buford gazed at her through his thick black-framed glasses. "I'm so happy," he whispered.

"Me too," she whispered back.

Buford cleared his throat. He held up his glass, signaling it was his time for a toast. The small crowd quieted. "Thank you for being here on such short notice. If this marriage came as a surprise to you, imagine what it is to me. I'm eighty-two and in love for the first time in my life. But, if I'm speaking the truth, I've been in love with Nora since the first time I saw her on TV. Something about her has always drawn my attention. Imagine my surprise when I saw her last night, asked to sit, and she said yes. Imagine my delight at our evening after. We spent the whole night walking around Vegas, talking, and sharing ice cream. I couldn't believe she was, is, as beautiful inside as she is out." He turned to Nora. "My love, you captured my heart long ago and I will forever be mesmerized by you. Thank you for being my wife."

Nora found herself speechless. Buford had real feelings for her.

Glasses clinked, everyone sipped, they shared another kiss. The conversation in the small crowd picked back up.

Nora was having second thoughts. This man deserved better than her. This could be annulled.

"Can we talk real quick?" she quietly asked and with a nod, Buford led her away from the table to a private corner.

She looked beyond his thick lenses and into his kind blue eyes. She couldn't believe what she was about to say. Call it conscience, or God's guilt, or the humbleness of the past year moving in, or Nora turning over yet another new leaf. She wasn't sure, but he needed to know.

"My mama told me to never marry a man who I loved more than he loved me. Unfortunately, that's the way it was with Merrell. Our life together was good, but it also made me bitter. I didn't get to be the person I wanted to be. I had to be someone others expected. In the end, it made me into a woman I wasn't proud of. I've done things I'm ashamed of. I want you to know that. I'm not this perfect trophy wife. I'm not arm candy. I'm intelligent, I'm funny, but I'm flawed. So very flawed. I've also lost everything. Merrell left his fortune to our daughter. Other than a small allowance, I have nothing. Now that I've married you, that allowance goes away. You need to know all of this and the fact I'm probably looking at some IRS issues as well. It's part of making amends, which if you don't know, I've been to rehab. You also seem clueless as to how bad my reputation has become. Do you not know what people say about me now?"

Buford's head tilted. He smiled. "I know you don't love me. That's okay. I know you've made mistakes. I know, too, everything else. It's okay. I want you to be honest and I want you to be yourself around me. That's it. That's all I want. If you'll let me, I'd love to spoil you rotten." He took her hand. "We are a total cliché—the old rich man and the gorgeous younger woman. But I don't care. I want you to show me your intellect. I want you to show me your humor. I also want to see your bad moods. Don't ever put on a show for me. Always be you. If you can put up with the gossip that will surround us, so can I."

Nora once again found herself speechless.

This man wanted her to be herself. Every ugly and pretty part about her, he wanted it. There had to be a catch. Didn't there?

He leaned in and this time she didn't mind the wet lips that touched hers.

"Okay," she quietly said. "Let's go back to the table and celebrate this union."

They returned to the party. She stood alongside Buford, smiling and laughing. Her phone rang and she saw her sponsor's name light up the screen.

She hit IGNORE and took another tiny sip of champagne.

Welcome back to the good life.

52

They'd been married four months and Buford stayed true to his word. He spoiled Nora rotten.

He ordered a custom-made Mercedes for her.

He bought her a villa in Italy.

He purchased her a brand new wardrobe.

His private jet sat waiting for her anytime she wanted to zip off.

He fulfilled her entire wish list of jewelry.

He even contracted a stylist to be on call if Nora woke up one morning and decided she wanted her hair straight, blown out, or wavy. Never hot rolled, though. Those days were happily behind her.

On Sundays they went to church. Nora wore a brand-new outfit for every single service. No one cared about her fall from glory, or they'd forgotten. Most were simply ecstatic that Nora Hodges attended the same service that they did.

Nora wished her mama was still alive so she could rub her nose in every single detail.

Nearly every day she texted Elizabeth with pictures of

her new things. At first, her daughter responded with a text back, but those became less frequent as the weeks and months transpired.

In July she took Buford to Palm Beach to see where it all started and to meet Elizabeth, of course.

Nora had called ahead so Raina could prepare for their arrival.

And now here she lounged on the terrace, talking on the phone while Buford did slow laps in the pool.

Nora said to one of her new Vegas friends, "I miss you too. I'll be here for the week at my old place and then back your way." She sat up. "Hey, how about we do a long weekend in Kauai?"

In her peripheral, she saw Elizabeth and Raina step through the sliding glass doors.

"Listen, let's chat later, my daughter just got here." She hung up and stood. "Elizabeth!" In high-heeled sandals, she crossed the short distance and wrapped her in a big hug. "I'm so excited to see you!"

Her daughter didn't hug her back.

Nora pulled away to survey her. She looked at her chest. "You have breasts. Amazing what four months can do to a body. Did you start your period too?"

Elizabeth fixed her with an indifferent stare.

Raina stepped forward, her hand extended. "Mrs. Hodges, good to see you."

"It's Mrs. Steele now."

"Mrs. Steele." Raina smiled politely.

Nora went back to Elizabeth. She didn't look happy. "What's wrong? Aren't you excited to see me?"

"What do you think, *Mother*?"

Nora took a shocked step back. What the heck?

Her daughter looked at Buford, still doing slow laps.

"You go off to Vegas to celebrate your birthday. You get married. You don't call me. Instead, I get text messages like you think that's communicating. Four months later and here you are." She folded her arms. "So, no, I'm not excited to see you."

Nora didn't know what to say. "I...I thought you'd be happy that I'm happy."

"Sure." Elizabeth shrugged. "Are you drinking again?"

"A little bit here and there. Nothing I can't control."

"So much for rehab."

"You watch your tone, young lady."

Raina cleared her throat.

Nora glared at Elizabeth. Elizabeth glared right back.

"Hi," Buford said.

Nora glanced over, getting a glimpse of his back hair as Buford stepped out of the water. He squinted at them, before reaching for his glasses sitting at the edge of the pool. He slipped them on, and with a warm and welcoming smile, he walked across the terrace.

"I'm Buford Steele." He held out a wet hand to Elizabeth first, then Raina. "It is so nice to meet both of you."

"What would you like for me to call you?" Elizabeth asked.

"Buford's fine." He took a towel off a nearby chair and dried his body. "Your father was an amazing man. I used to watch him on TV. I'm honored to be here in his home and to meet his daughter."

A small smile began to curve Elizabeth's face. "Thank you."

"I'd love for all of us to be friends." He looked between her and Raina. "Does that sound good?"

"Of course, that sounds good," Raina said and Elizabeth slowly nodded.

Buford motioned to a nearby table. "Why don't we all sit and chat."

Raina went inside to get everyone a beverage. Buford and Elizabeth sat across from each other at the table. And Nora stood awkwardly watching her daughter and husband talk.

None of them looked her way once.

∼

Buford spent every available minute getting to know Nora's daughter.

They played in the ocean.

They ventured into town.

They set off fireworks on the Fourth of July.

They challenged each other to various board games.

Nora tried to insert herself a few times, but Elizabeth's cold shoulder toward her grew more and more frigid.

Her daughter had become an icy bitch.

53

The next few months rolled by and Nora threw herself into redoing Buford's seven-thousand-square-foot condo in Vegas. She tore out the walls to open things up. She got rid of all the old furniture and bought all new ones. She replaced the cabinetry. She ripped out the dated bathroom fixtures. She repainted. She took up the hardwood floors and laid down tile.

Nora liked to tell people she did this, and she did that, but of course, she did nothing. She hired and coordinated crews.

She worked with an architect. She consulted with a decorator.

She paid extra money to have things done quickly.

She inquired about the condo next door because wouldn't it be great to own both and connect them? But so far the couple who owned it wasn't willing to sell. That's okay, everyone had a price. Nora just needed to figure out theirs.

Either that or she would talk Buford into buying the penthouse. It's where Nora would rather be anyway.

She stood looking out over the city and sipping her daily allotted four-ounce glass of vodka as the workers packed up for the day. The architect approached. Nora nodded to the Vegas view blocked by a half-wall that separated the living room from the balcony. "Can we take that out? I mean, what is the purpose of the half-wall? I'd like to be able to see the whole strip unobstructed. I want the living room to flow out onto the balcony."

The architect made a note. "It shouldn't be an issue."

The front door opened and in walked Buford with Elizabeth and Raina, having picked them up at the private airport where he kept his jet.

Buford had insisted they spend Christmas with Elizabeth. "Your daughter is turning thirteen. You have to celebrate that with her."

"Of course," Nora had responded. But after the way her daughter treated her in July, Nora could happily go another year without laying eyes on her.

"I'm so happy you two are here," Buford said to them. "Vegas is amazing. I can't wait to show you around."

"Thank you again for sending your plane," Raina said. "That was very thoughtful of you."

"Oh, sure." He waved that off.

Elizabeth paused in the entryway, looking around the construction zone before meeting Nora's gaze. Her daughter's eyes fell straight to the vodka Nora held.

She downed it, just because she could.

"Don't worry," Nora said. "We made sure your bed and bath were done first." Actually, Buford made sure. Her eyes met Raina's next and they exchanged a nod.

Buford rolled a suitcase across the condo. "The guest room has twin beds. I'm assuming you're okay to share?"

"Yes, not a problem," Raina told him.

As the two of them followed him into the guest room, Nora went back to watching the workers pack up. A few minutes later, Elizabeth came up beside her, and together they stood looking out over the twinkle lit city.

"It's pretty," Elizabeth commented, her tone flat.

"Yes, it is," Nora replied, her tone just as flat.

Thanksgiving was the last time they had been in contact, not by either one of their choices. Buford called and put Elizabeth on speaker. They'd said exactly five words.

Elizabeth: Happy Thanksgiving, Mother.

Nora: You too.

She took a second to study her daughter's reflection in the floor to ceiling windows recently installed. She wore her dark hair down and it flowed over a red cropped sweater. Gray leggings led to black ballet flats. "How tall are you now?"

"Five-eight. Raina says I'm still growing and will be tall like Daddy."

"Hm." Nora rotated away from the view. "Shall we sit?" She led the way over to a white L-shaped linen sofa.

Buford came down the hall with Raina. He went into the kitchen while she veered off into the bathroom. "Elizabeth, would you like something to drink? We have soda, juice, water, milk…"

Elizabeth opened her mouth to respond and Nora murmured, "You get my brand new sofa dirty and I won't be happy."

Her daughter didn't miss a beat. "Coke if you have it," she called out.

Nora's eyes narrowed.

Elizabeth looked again at the empty tumbler. "I'm assuming that wasn't water."

"You assume correctly." Nora fished a piece of ice out and loudly crunched it.

While Buford went about filling two glasses, Nora and Elizabeth sat silent, waiting on him to join them. When he finally did, he gave Elizabeth her Coke, placed a second glass on a coaster, and took a seat between them on the L-shaped couch.

Raina joined them, taking the cushion beside Elizabeth. Her appearance visibly relaxed Elizabeth, and that pleased Nora.

Her daughter wasn't so unaffected by her after all.

Ain't nothing wrong with some healthy fear, her mama would have said.

How very true.

With a smile for Nora's daughter, Buford said, "Maybe we can all go to church together while you're here."

Elizabeth looked right at Nora. "You go to church?"

"Of course, I go to church."

"Could've fooled me," she murmured.

Buford cleared his throat. Raina put her hand on Elizabeth's knee. And Nora got up for a second vodka. Her daughter was driving her to drink.

"What have you been up to?" Buford asked. "Are you still at the same school?"

"I am." Elizabeth gave him her full attention. "I love my friends and teachers. I love Dr. Wong, she's the director and also the school counselor. I finished the mentor-in-training program and became an actual mentor at the start of the new school year. Oh, I also began playing soccer!" Elizabeth grinned. "My academy is too small to have a team but we have a sister school where I play. My coach says I'm good. Uncle Cooper and Uncle Hudson come to nearly every game."

Raina chimed in, "She is really good."

"Uncle Cooper says if I keep it up, I might score an athletic scholarship in a few years when I'm ready for college."

"That's great!" Buford exclaimed. He looked over at Nora. "We should go to a game sometime."

"Mm." Nora squeezed a lime down over the fresh drink.

"What else?" Buford asked with genuine interest.

"I've been working and saving money. It's just in the cafeteria at school, but Uncle Hudson says it's important to develop a work ethic. I know I have an inheritance but I don't want to take it for granted."

Buford beamed a proud smile at Nora who took her time in the kitchen recapping the vodka and placing the bottle in the freezer. "You have some daughter here, Nora. You should be proud."

"Yep." Nora closed the freezer door.

"What about subjects? How are you doing in school?" Buford asked.

Elizabeth cringed. "I'm not a very good student."

"Don't." Gently, Raina squeezed her knee. "She studies hard. I've seen it time and again."

Buford leaned in. "I didn't make A's either. Studying doesn't come easy for everyone. The important thing is that you *do* study. Never stop applying yourself."

"Studying came easy for me." Nora crossed back over to the sofa. "I can read a page and remember every single detail. I think I have a photographic memory." She sat back down. "I guess you don't get your intellect from me then."

All three of them ignored her.

Buford looked at Raina. "What about you? What have you been up to?"

"Elizabeth typically spends every weekend at home. My

sister's daughter is a year younger. We generally plan things with them. Other than that..."

Raina kept talking, eventually cycling the conversation back to Elizabeth. Nora listened for as long as she could. What exactly was so intriguing about school, soccer, and Raina's niece?

Uncle Cooper this. Uncle Hudson that. Raina. Raina. Raina.

Nora had enough. She left them talking and went onto the balcony to have a cigarette.

Leaning against the Plexiglas railing, Nora took a drag. She looked out over the city before peering forty-six floors down to the busy street below.

She had a quick image of herself falling over, her scream echoing in the night as her body plummeted toward earth. Nora saw herself looking up to find Elizabeth on the balcony staring down. The wind whipped her daughter's long dark hair around her red sweater. Nora reached out a hand beckoning her daughter to save her, but Elizabeth didn't move.

The visceral vision shocked Nora and she shoved away from the railing. Her pulse raced.

She whipped around, looking back into the condo. Raina said something and Buford chuckled. Elizabeth, though, sat staring at Nora through unflinching eyes. Something shifted in her daughter's gaze—a darkness, a hatred, a desire for vengeance—as if she knew what Nora had just imagined and hoped it would come true.

54

Christmas week went by much like that week in July. Buford, Elizabeth, and Raina did everything together and Nora stayed out of their way.

She'd like to think nothing scared her, but somehow one vision and look from Elizabeth had.

Nora was officially creeped out by her daughter.

When it came time to say goodbye, she gave Elizabeth a brief hug—mainly because Buford and Raina stood there—and left her husband to see them off. The next time he insisted she visit with her daughter, Nora would find an excuse. Hell, she'd pretend to have cancer if need be.

Now it was the New Year, and Nora found Buford in the home office, thoughtfully studying a spreadsheet on the computer.

She pressed a kiss to his bald head. "I need retail therapy. I'll be back later."

With a sigh, Buford sat back in his chair. He took his thick-framed glasses off and rubbed his eyes.

Nora looked between him and the computer. She didn't

care about what was going on, but she thought asking would be the kind, wifely thing to do. She propped her hip on the desk. "What's up?"

"You have no idea how much I hate what I'm about to say." He stopped rubbing his eyes. "You—*we've* got to cut back on money. We haven't even been married a year yet and we've blown through more cash in that time than I have in—"

"What are you talking about?" Nora waved her arm around the under-construction home office. "We both decided to redo your condo. Do you have any idea how stressful this has been for me? I'm basically living in sawdust right now. I offered to reserve us a suite somewhere until the condo was done, but you didn't want to."

"I know, and I appreciate all your hard work coordinating work crews and such, but—"

"But what Buford?" Nora pushed off from the desk. "If you intended on marrying me and putting me in some low-income situation like I grew up in, then you better think again. I'm only moving up in this world."

Buford tried again, reaching for her hand. She allowed him to take it. "That's not what I'm saying. It's my greatest joy to spoil you and give you everything you want. But, a few things here and there will help. Like the impromptu weekend trips to Hawaii. If we don't cut back on some things, we'll run out of money."

"Run out of money?" She took her hand from his. "That sounds like your problem, not mine. You're the businessman. I'm the 'arm candy' you trot around. You wanted Nora Hodges, your long time crush? Well, this is me. Pay the price."

For several beats, he stared at her as if he couldn't wrap

his brain around what she'd just said. Fine, it was time for her to stop filtering her words. He wanted the true her. Well, then, here she was.

"I have never once thought of you as 'arm candy,'" he said. "That was your term, not mine. You're letting your temper get the best of you. Be reasonable. I have given you everything and more without a blink of an eye. I even handled your IRS issues. I'm only asking we make a few adjustments here and there."

"As I said, you're the businessman." She leaned in. "Figure. It. Out."

Buford slid his glasses back on. He pushed back from the desk and stood. His tone was no longer gentle and reasonable. "I *have* figured it out. Do you want me to put a hold on the credit cards you're about to go burn through?"

Nora saw red.

"I didn't think so."

"I expect to live a certain way." She lifted her chin.

"That way you expect to live is breaking my bank."

"You should have thought of that before you said you wanted to spoil me. I took that literally. Why should I suffer because you can't manage money?"

Buford huffed a laugh. "Suffer? You really feel as if you 'suffer?' I didn't think the rumors were true. I gave you the benefit of the doubt." He looked her up and down. "This woman standing in front of me is not the woman I harbored a longtime crush on. This woman is disappointing."

He took a couple of deep breaths, pushing the heel of his hand into his chest. Sweat beaded his brow. He sat back down.

"What's wrong with you?" Nora snapped.

"Nothing." He slid open a desk drawer and brought out a pill bottle. "Just leave me alone."

"Fine." Nora folded her arms. "I will."

She went straight for the vodka. Now Buford was the one driving her to drink.

55

On their first anniversary, Buford wasn't feeling well. Nora's new Vegas friends were spending a long weekend in New York. Just because her husband was sick, didn't mean she should pass up an opportunity to have fun.

Been there done that with Merrell. She wouldn't be tending to another husband's sickly needs.

Nora didn't ask. She told Buford that she was going. After all, it was her forty-ninth birthday as well.

To her surprise, he didn't care. He insisted she go have fun.

So, she did.

The women hopped a private jet, and off they went for a long weekend. On the morning they were scheduled to fly back to Vegas, Nora's buzzing phone woke her up.

"What?" she grumbled.

"Mrs. Steele, this is Dr. Vader, your husband's cardiologist."

It took Nora a moment to remember she was Mrs. Steele now, not Mrs. Hodges. "Yes?"

"I've been taking care of Buford for years. I'm so sorry to have to tell you that your husband suffered a heart attack. We did everything we could to save him, but he died."

∼

Dressed in all black, Nora sat across from Buford's lawyer. She had a quick image of this same scene years ago with Hudson and Cooper.

Except for this time, things would be different.

There was no heir to swoop in and take her money. Buford had never been married before and never had children. Nora was set to inherit it all.

A gleaming mahogany desk separated her from the lawyer. She concentrated on maintaining the manner of a suffering, saintly widow.

"My condolences," the lawyer said. "Buford Steele was an amazing man. Intelligent, forward-thinking, and kind. He would have done anything for anyone. I've known Buford a long time and though your time with him was brief, you were there to share in his burdens and joys."

Nora bowed her head, fighting tears.

A beat went by. The lawyer delicately cleared his throat. "I want to give you ample time to transition…"

Slowly, Nora's head came up. Her tears dried. Her eyes narrowed.

"Buford's holdings need to be liquidated to pay his debts. The casino boats. His shares here in Vegas. The condo the two of you recently redid. The jet. The villa in Italy. The Mercedes. The jewelry—"

Nora held up a hand. She kept her voice calm. "I knew Buford was financially struggling, but he never told me he was upside down."

Solemnly, the lawyer nodded. "Buford borrowed against everything he owned to stay afloat."

"I'm not some poor little widow that you can take advantage of." Nora leaned forward. "My name is on the villa. My name is on the Mercedes. I own my jewelry."

With no emotion, the lawyer looked back at her. "Can you afford to keep those items? Because none of them are paid for."

Her anger built. "I want to see the papers. I want you to prove to me that what you're saying is true."

"As a longtime friend of Buford's, I appreciate your devotion to him during the last year of his life. You made him very happy." The lawyer linked fingers on top of the desk in a move straight out of a TV show. "It'll take some time, but I can put together the paperwork you are requesting."

She stood up. "This isn't happening to me again. I've spent my life fighting and clawing for what I want. For what I deserve. I won't be screwed by another husband."

"Mrs. Steele, I don't want any hard feelings. I respected your husband. And I know how much you meant to him. Buford certainly didn't intend to 'screw' you out of anything. He would've left you the world if possible."

"Any hard feelings?" Nora scoffed. "I plan on contesting this."

"That's fine, but I assure you, you won't be able to find a lawyer who will take this on contingency. One look at the papers and they'll know they can't win."

"We'll see about that. You forget who I am." She lifted a chin. "I am Nora Hodges. That name has power."

His reply came gently. "Not anymore."

56

Nora let herself into the Palm Beach home and stood for a moment, feeling the heaviness of the walls pushing in. This was the absolute last place she wanted to be, but where she always ended up.

At least she didn't have some viral sex video driving her back this time.

She looked up the stairs and sighed.

Laughter filtered over from the kitchen as she placed her suitcase in the foyer. She followed the voices to find Elizabeth and Raina making salads.

Simultaneously, they glanced up.

Elizabeth blinked. She glanced beyond her as if looking for Buford. "I didn't realize you two were coming for a visit."

Nora looked around the familiar kitchen, feeling comfort and nostalgia she hadn't expected. "Buford died."

Raina gasped. Elizabeth stared.

"In March. Just after our first anniversary." She took a step forward.

"It's...July." Elizabeth looked at Raina, confused.

"I know. I've been handling things. Legal things."

"I'm sorry, Mrs. Hod—Steele." Raina frowned. "If we would've known…"

"I liked Buford," Elizabeth murmured. "I'm so sorry."

She accepted the condolence with true gratefulness. "Thank you."

A few awkward seconds went by as the three of them stood there, not sure what to say or do.

Surreptitiously, Nora glanced over to the wall-mounted key hook to see her old Mercedes fob still hanging there. Good.

She slid onto a stool as she eyed the salads. "I haven't eaten all day. Mind if I make one?"

"Of course." Raina scooted the containers of already cut vegetables over to Nora and then got her a plate.

With a sigh, she looked around the kitchen again. "I forgot how much I love this place."

Neither of them responded.

Nora took her time creating a bed of green lettuce. She weighed the next couple of minutes, strategizing her words. She wished she had slammed some vodka before coming in here.

She stopped with the lettuce and retrieved her purse from where she'd looped it on the stool's back. She opened it and brought out a white jewelry box. "I got this for you as an apology. You're right. I married Buford and got caught up in his fancy life. I neglected you. I'm sorry."

Nora slid the box over and watched as Elizabeth opened the lid. Inside sat a white gold band with a turquoise stone.

Surprise lit her daughter's eyes. "That's my birthstone."

"I know." Nora smiled.

Actually, she didn't know. Buford had bought it for Elizabeth. Nora found it when she was cleaning out their Vegas condo. It came attached to a card he'd written:

Just because...
Love, Buford

But with everything that happened, he never had a chance to send it.

Nora had planned on hocking it, but at the last moment, decided it would serve a better purpose. It would be her ticket back into this place.

Now the card read:

Just because...
Love, Mother

"Thank you," Elizabeth said, but she didn't put it on. "And thank you for the apology."

"You're welcome." Nora went back to assembling her salad, eyeing her daughter as she studied the ring. The last time she saw her, Nora got a creepy vibe. Right now that vibe wasn't there.

Elizabeth seemed more thoughtful than anything.

"How are things at school?" Nora searched her brain, trying to remember the questions Buford asked. "Soccer still going good?"

"Yes."

"She's being moved to varsity," Raina said.

Nora smiled. "That's great, Elizabeth. I'm proud of you. I hope we can—"

"When was the last time you had a drink?"

"The day Buford passed," Nora lied.

"Are you back in the program?"

"Yes," she lied again.

"Good."

With a small smile, Raina slid the Italian dressing over to her.

Unlike the last time she crawled home looking for a roof over her head, there was no emotional hugging or crying.

She treaded carefully, moving the conversation through school, friends, and soccer. She concentrated on listening and absorbing. She made all the appropriate comments, asked questions that focused solely on Elizabeth, and brought Raina into the conversation here and there.

Did she have an interest in any of it? No, but that wasn't the point.

The point was to appear attentive and in the moment.

They ate their salads. They cleaned the kitchen together. The scene played out better than Nora expected. So perfectly in fact, that no one blinked when she took her suitcase upstairs and unpacked.

57

The rest of the summer went by without incident. Nora concentrated on Elizabeth and being the best damn parent she could before her daughter went back to school. They swam in the ocean. They played games. They made meals, binge-watched TV, and Elizabeth taught Nora soccer.

All the while, Raina carefully watched, ready to intercede if need be. But Nora worked hard to prove herself. She considered the goal accomplished when Raina left them unsupervised to run an errand.

Granted it was only twenty minutes, but still. She knew Raina and Cooper talked and she needed Raina to give her a perfect report card.

By the end of August, Nora had crammed a lifetime of mother/daughter bonding into the summer. She'd convinced herself Elizabeth held no deviant and dark ill-wishes toward her. She and her daughter were fine.

On the last day, Cooper showed up.

Nora sat on the terrace steps, watching Elizabeth bodyboard in the ocean.

Cooper took the spot beside her. "Nora."

"Cooper."

"What do you want?" He got right to the point.

Nora didn't look at him. She kept watching Elizabeth. "To spend time with my daughter."

"I heard Buford died."

"Yes."

"I also heard you're broke."

"You hear a lot of things."

"Legally, I can't give you the allowance again. That stopped when you remarried."

"I know."

"I'll repeat my first question then. What do you want?"

Still, Nora didn't look at him. "To move back in. I have no other place to go."

"Fine," Cooper quickly replied as if he had been expecting her words. "Move back in. But these are the rules. Elizabeth boards at Care and Hope during the weekdays and comes home nearly every weekend. You will be sober and involved, and I will ask Raina every Monday morning for a report." He stood back up. "You lay one hand on her, and you're done. You understand me?"

"Yes."

"Raina operates off of a household budget. I'll increase it accordingly for you. We go to church every Sunday. You're welcome to join us. Ferris has been doing a fabulous job. You would be impressed."

"Nobody wants to see me back at that church."

"Your decision. But you need to think about your future. Elizabeth is not responsible for you."

Why not? Nora had taken care of Mama. It's what a daughter was supposed to do. There was nothing wrong with that cycle.

"You've got a college education. Do something with it other than marry another rich husband."

Another husband. Now there was a thought. Talk about cycles.

"You're capable of so much more than lying around here and pickling your liver."

"I haven't been drinking."

"Good." With that, he walked down to the ocean to say hi to Elizabeth.

"Tell them what they want to hear," she murmured.

58

Elizabeth went back to Care and Hope, officially a freshman in high school. Nora and Raina fell into a routine. Raina would rise early, do errands, clean, cook, and on her downtime, she'd read. Nora would sleep in, work out, eat, shower, and attend a daily AA meeting.

Every night she'd say goodnight, lock her bedroom door, and drink herself to sleep with the stash she hid in a shoebox. It was the best part of the whole day.

Every weekend Elizabeth came home and Nora focused on being sober super-mom. She considered Friday through Sunday her work hours where she earned her room and board. She didn't drink on those days and told herself that meant she wasn't an alcoholic. If she were a true alcoholic, then she'd need to drink every day.

She couldn't bring herself to show her face in church. Instead, she had her own church at the house where she read the Bible, analyzed her actions, and prayed for forgiveness. Like Step Ten on repeat.

True to his word, Cooper called every Monday morning to find out how the weekend went.

Nora's world had become one giant Groundhog's Day.

On a Wednesday afternoon in October, Nora got a head start on the best part of her day. Raina wouldn't be home until late. Nora had the whole place to herself.

Carrying her fourth—or maybe fifth—vodka, she held tight to the banister, and slowly descended the stairs. "One. Two. Three..." She counted the steps out loud. It helped her focus on not missing one. Maybe they should invest in one of those chairs that moved up and down.

Something to think about it.

She found Raina in the kitchen, watching an iPad.

Nora hid the glass behind her back and concentrated on not slurring her words. "What are you doing here?"

"My appointment got canceled." She pointed to the screen. "Cooper's live streaming Elizabeth's soccer game."

Nora leaned in, squinting at the screen. She couldn't tell which one was Elizabeth. They all looked the same in their uniforms and ponytails. While Raina kept watching, Nora slid onto a stool next to her and leaned so far toward her that their shoulders pressed together.

Raina glanced over. "Have you been drinking?"

"No." She smiled.

Through the iPad speakers, the crowd cheered. A bunch of girls leaped up and high-fived each other. Nora's eyes closed. She laid her head on Raina's shoulder.

Raina sighed. "I'll deal with you later. I don't want to miss the game."

"Okay." Nora nodded.

"There she is!" Raina clapped.

Nora cringed.

"Go! Go! Go! Yes!"

The crowd cheered again and Nora pried her eyelids back open. On the screen the entire team of girls surrounded Elizabeth, lifting her on their shoulders. Her daughter looked happy, popular, pretty. It made Nora proud.

"She got the winning goal! Isn't that fabulous?" Raina reached for her cell. Nora had no clue who she was texting. Elizabeth. Cooper. Hudson. Maybe all three.

"I played softball," Nora said. "I was good. She gets her athletic ability from me."

Raina barely acknowledged her as she fired off another text.

Nora went back to watching the tiny screen. She had to admit, her daughter was impressive.

Wait a minute...

Leaning in, she studied the girls now down on the ground. One of them curled into a tight ball and held her stomach. The coach rushed in.

"Raina." She grabbed her arm. "Raina." She shook her. "Raina."

"What?" Raina snapped.

Nora jabbed her finger on the screen. "Elizabeth's hurt. Something's wrong."

59

Raina walked quickly into the hospital and Nora followed at a slower pace. While Raina checked the text Cooper just sent, Nora finished off the Coke that she'd quickly grabbed from the refrigerator.

"Can I help you?" An elderly man behind a help desk asked.

"Yes, we need pediatric surgery," Raina said.

The man pointed to the elevator. "Second floor, take a left."

Nora tossed her empty can in a recycle bin, fished a piece of gum from her purse, and then popped that in her mouth. While she chewed, she trailed after Raina, into the elevator, up and out, and down the hall.

They walked into a waiting room decorated with a mural of multicolored dancing bunnies.

Pacing the small area, Cooper stopped when he saw them. "They rushed her straight in. She got hit in the liver, didn't even realize it. They're sealing off the blood vessels. But she had a lot of internal bleeding. She needs a transfusion. Hudson got here about ten minutes ago. He matched perfectly with AB negative. He's donating right now."

"Oh my God." Raina hugged Cooper. "I'm so glad you were there."

"Me too." He held her tight. "The surgeon assured me everything will be okay but I won't breathe until I see Elizabeth out and in recovery."

Nora blew a bubble. Her eyes crossed at the big pink pillow expanding in front of her face. She hated the color pink.

"Is she drunk?"

"Yes," Raina sighed, taking Nora's shoulder and pushing her into a chair. "Let me go find some coffee and food to sober her up."

Raina left and Cooper didn't say a word, he simply glared at her.

Nora smiled as the gum popped.

"You're unbelievable," he said.

"I know, right?"

∽

NORA DOZED IN AND OUT. She heard voices, making out *surgery went well* and *six weeks to recover* and *she's being moved to room 215.*

She smacked her lips and resituated herself.

A little while later she heard *there are so many tubes* and *she's so pale* and *the coach is here.*

The sound of feet shuffled in and out.

What do you want to do with Nora?

Just leave her there.

The waiting room fell silent and she drifted further into oblivion. Her mouth felt dry. A headache was forming. She wished Elizabeth or Raina had made her the ultimate hangover cure.

Someone shoved her shoulder. "Wake the hell up."

Nora's eyes slit open. Dancing bunnies greeted her. She stared at them. Where was she?

Hudson moved into her line of sight. His dark hair looked disheveled. He wore a white dress shirt, rolled up on the right side with white gauze around his elbow.

She smiled. When was the last time she saw Hudson? She looked at the dancing bunnies again, the empty padded chairs, and up to the wall-mounted clock that read 10:00. Would that be a.m. or p.m.?

"You're in the same waiting room you've been in for hours," Hudson said as if reading her thoughts.

Waiting room... She looked at his arm again. "Are you hurt?"

"Jesus Christ!" His jaw clenched. He shoved his hands into his trouser pockets. He paced the small room.

Nora didn't know what his problem was, but her head was killing her. She saw her purse shoved down next to her and dug inside. She found a Snickers bar that Raina must have put there. That would be good later, but she wanted Advil. She kept digging.

"Is she mine?" Hudson demanded.

Nora had no clue what he was talking about. She kept digging through her purse. "Will you get me something to drink? My head is killing me. I need Advil too."

"No, I won't get you something to drink!"

She cringed. "Why are you yelling?"

Cooper walked in. He looked right at Nora. "Good, you're up." He handed her water and Tylenol. "Take this, then go wash your face with cold water. You need to see your daughter."

Nora stood. "What is going on?"

"Elizabeth just had major surgery," Cooper said in a measured tone. "Now sober up and come with me."

Nora grabbed her purse and stood. She looked at Hudson and his jaw tightened. She didn't know what his problem was, but he needed to get over it.

60

The nurses saw Nora like that, the doctors, Elizabeth's coach, girls from the soccer team, and other various people. In the past, Nora would have cared. She'd have been embarrassed, or made up an excuse, or lied her way out of it.

Now, she shrugged. It's what people expected of her.

"You can either check yourself into rehab again or you can move out. What's it going to be, Nora?" Cooper asked.

"Rehab."

"Good choice."

Unlike the last time Nora went to rehab, this time she put no effort into the program. She did her requirements and counted down the time until her ninety days were up.

Elizabeth recovered from surgery as a homebound student. Raina brought her once a week on family visitation day to see Nora.

On an early morning in January, Nora walked from the facility and straight toward Raina's SUV. Elizabeth sat in the front seat and Nora climbed into the back.

With a smile, her daughter looked over the seat. "I'm proud of you, Mother."

"Thanks."

"What do you want to do on your first day of freedom?" she joked.

Drink, Nora thought, but she smiled right back. "How about shopping? I missed your fourteenth birthday. You can probably use some new school clothes."

"That sounds fun."

"It does," Raina agreed.

The whole way home, Nora stared out the window, strategizing how to better drink this time around.

It was as they were pulling back into the estate, that Raina's phone rang. She frowned. "It's my father."

She answered it, greeting her dad in Spanish. Nora and Elizabeth climbed from Raina's SUV. But Raina didn't move from the driver's seat. She switched the call off Bluetooth and listened intently, her ear pressed firmly to her cell.

"What do you think's going on?" Nora mumbled to Elizabeth.

"I don't know. Her dad rarely calls her though. Something must be wrong."

Raina started shouting then. It was so loud, her voice boomed through the closed SUV doors.

Nora and Elizabeth both winced.

The yelling went on for several minutes before Raina finally hung up. She stepped from the vehicle and slammed the door. "My grandmother passed away and my father told the hospital just to put her in a pauper's grave." Raina charged past them. "I'm going to pack a bag. I have to go."

She let herself into the house.

Overhead the sun shifted, tucking behind a cloud. A balmy South Florida wind kicked in and Nora glanced up, noting dark lines slowly moving in from the ocean. For January, it seemed warmer than usual.

"Is it supposed to rain?" Elizabeth asked, looking up too.

Nora shrugged. "Don't know, but what do you say we still go shopping?"

"Maybe ice cream too?"

"It's a plan." Nora's phone rang. "Cooper," she answered.

"Raina just called me and told me what's going on. I don't want you alone with Elizabeth, but I can't leave work, and neither can Hudson."

Nora turned away from her daughter so she couldn't hear Cooper's voice. "Elizabeth and I are going shopping. We'll be back later. Everything is fine."

Cooper hesitated. "I'm going to call every hour. And know that either myself or Hudson will be stopping by to check on Elizabeth. By then I'll have a plan in place to cover for Raina being gone."

She rolled her eyes. "Whatever you feel is best."

Another gust rolled in from the ocean as Nora hung up. She looked again to the sky, gradually growing darker.

That's an omen if I've ever seen one, her mama would've said.

61

Nora and Elizabeth spent hours shopping. They hit several stores. Elizabeth tried on a zillion things. They ate lunch followed by ice cream.

Surprisingly, Nora didn't think once about drinking.

It was late afternoon when they pulled back into the garage. The sky continued to cling gloomy and heavy, threatening the slow-moving storm.

Elizabeth opened the passenger door. "I'm going to put on one of my new swimsuits and hit the pool before the rain comes."

"Sounds great." Nora trailed behind, helping her daughter carry in the bags of new clothes.

In the kitchen, Raina had taped a note to the microwave. *I threw together a crockpot before I left. I'll call once I know more.*

Nora checked the pot and inhaled. Yum. She loved Raina's garlic turkey and mushroom soup.

For now, though, she made a quick snack of celery and hummus and was just about to eat when her daughter came in dressed in a pink athletic bikini and matching long sleeve rash guard.

She didn't realize she'd bought that one.

Grinning, Elizabeth spun a circle. "What do you think?"

Like a switch had been flipped, Nora's good mood instantly darkened. Images flashed across her eyes—a pink negligee, a pink party dress, a pink little girl's room, a pink butterfly pendant, a pink evening gown, a gaudy pink business suit, pink lipstick... Pink. Pink. PINK. "I *hate* pink."

Elizabeth's grin slowly faded. "Oh."

Nora swiped celery through hummus. "Pink's a horrible color for you."

Silence.

Nora crunched.

Elizabeth self-consciously looked down at the suit. "Raina says I look good in pink."

"What does Raina know? She's a maid."

Elizabeth brought her gaze back up. Nora crunched more celery.

"Well, I bought it with my own money, so I'm keeping it."

Nora snorted. "Yes, we're all fully aware you're the one with the money in this house." She swiveled away from the kitchen island and over to the freezer. She opened the bottom drawer, looking for vodka before remembering there would be none there.

From beside the refrigerator, she got the stepladder. Using it, she reached up to the top cabinet and grabbed the cooking sherry.

Quietly, Elizabeth watched her unscrew the lid and guzzle the entire bottle. She grabbed the red wine next, laughing when she found a bottle of rum in the cabinet's corner. Raina's cooking stash.

Carrying both, she climbed down from the ladder and brushed past her daughter to go upstairs.

On the landing, she paused, listening to Elizabeth slide

open the glass door to the terrace. Nora wedged the cork from the red wine and gulped it as she strolled into her daughter's bedroom. She found her new clothes laid out on her bed, still with the tags. She selected a white bikini and set it aside with the rum. The rest she scooped up and carrying the wine, took the pile down to the laundry room. She put them all in the slop sink and as she drank the rest of the wine, she poured an entire gallon of bleach down over them.

Humming now, she went back into the kitchen. Outside on the terrace, Elizabeth sat on the side of the pool with her legs dangling in the heated water. She stared out at the dark sky.

Nora tossed the wine bottle in the recycle bin. It clinked against the sherry. She swayed. She laughed.

Back upstairs again, she put on Elizabeth's new white bikini, tags and all. She found white stilettos in her master closet and put them on.

Carrying the rum, she carefully descended the steps, counting her way back down. "One, two, three..." In the kitchen, she paused long enough to unscrew the lid and toss it into the sink. She swayed again. Too bad it wasn't vodka, but God, she'd missed this oblivion.

She opened the sliding glass door and stepped outside.

Elizabeth glanced over her shoulder and froze.

With her chest out and chin up, Nora strolled the terrace. She paused at the steps that led down to the sand to gaze out at the rough water. The stormy sky tilted and for a moment she thought it wasn't real. Then it righted itself and she smirked.

She turned around, catching Elizabeth still staring at her with a sort of horrified fascination. "What are you looking at?" Nora snapped.

"That's one of my new bikinis."

"Yeah, so?" She tipped the rum bottle up. After a swallow, she concentrated on not catching her stiletto as she walked another lap around the stone terrace.

It began to sprinkle.

When she circled behind Elizabeth, her daughter's shoulders tensed and Nora sneered.

She rounded the pool and caught Elizabeth looking nervously over her shoulder back toward the house.

"What?" Nora took a step forward. "You scared to be out here with me?"

"No." Elizabeth swallowed.

Nora squinted. She took another drink, pleased to see how full the bottle still was. "Yes, you are. You look shaky as hell over there." She pointed the bottle at her. "You're the reason I drink. My whole world was perfect until you."

Her daughter pulled her legs out of the water and stood. "I'm going in."

"Your father made me wear pink when he wanted to fuck."

Elizabeth gasped.

The sprinkles turned to rain.

Nora brought the rum to her lips. She swayed.

Is she mine?

Hudson's words from the hospital came back to her. She'd forgotten all about that until this moment.

The rain increased, but neither of them moved. With the pool between them, she stared at her daughter. Merrell and Hudson were both tall with brown hair and eyes. But where Merrell's skin tone had been lighter, Hudson was more olive complected.

Like Elizabeth.

Where Merrell's eyes were large and alert, Hudson's tipped down on the corners.

Like Elizabeth.

Merrell had a straight nose. Hudson's had a bump.

Like Elizabeth.

Merrell had O positive blood. Hudson had AB negative.

Like Elizabeth.

And where Merrell's body ran on the lean side, Hudson's was more muscular.

Like Elizabeth.

"Oh my God!" Nora laughed. "You're not even his."

Elizabeth didn't respond.

Nora pointed across the pool at her daughter. "Merrell's not even your daddy!"

"Wh-what are you talking about?"

"It's Hudson!" Nora hooted.

Elizabeth's eyes blurred with tears. "That's not true."

"It is!" Nora slapped her thigh and rainwater flung from her fingers. She danced in place. "This is too great."

Her daughter's bottom lip wobbled. "That's a lie."

"Oh, boo-hoo." Nora leaned forward. "Looks like your perfect little world isn't so perfect, huh?"

"I hate you!" Elizabeth screamed.

Thunder shook the sky. The wind whistled.

"Back at you!" She chucked the bottle at Elizabeth and it missed her to shatter across the wet terrace. Nora charged around the pool. Her stiletto caught in the seam between two stones and she lost her balance. She went down hard, her head bouncing off the side of the pool, and she rolled into the water.

Blood surrounded her.

She fought to the surface, gasping for air. "Help me!"

Elizabeth didn't move. The wind picked at her long dark

hair, sending wet tendrils up into the air. She stayed several feet away, staring down at Nora. Something shifted in her daughter's gaze—a darkness, a hatred, a desire for vengeance—and Nora was reminded of that same look Elizabeth had in Vegas.

Her head slipped beneath the water again. She thrashed. More blood flowed. Rain pattered. Through the blurriness, she saw her daughter still standing there, not moving. Nora kicked and paddled. Her head once again surfaced. She sucked in more water than air. She reached a hand out to her daughter.

But Elizabeth still didn't move.

Nora's head fuzzed. Her lungs burned. The world went in and out.

Nothing should ever stop you, not even me.

Her words to Elizabeth from years ago floated through her brain. And as she slipped under the water for the last time, her daughter's voice was the last thing she heard.

"Mother, may I be free?"

EPILOGUE
TWENTY YEARS LATER

Baltimore, Maryland

Elizabeth sat on a park bench beside Hudson, watching her six-year-old daughter play.

"Grandpa!" her daughter, Sarah, yelled. "Look!"

She slid down a slide with her hands in the air. "No hands!"

Hudson waved. "I see!"

Giggling, she skipped off to play with other children.

"She's going to be athletic, like you." Hudson laughed. "That girl is always hanging upside down or running headlong into whatever."

Elizabeth nodded. "She drives her daddy nuts."

"When will he be back?"

"Day after tomorrow. I'm excited to see him. He travels so much with work. Our time is few and far right now. But I'm proud of him."

"As you should be." Hudson smiled at her. "I'm proud of how hard both of you work."

"Thank you, Dad." Though she'd been working as a mental health counselor for children, she'd only recently opened her own office.

Hudson slid his hand inside his right coat pocket and brought out a silver jewelry box. He wedged the lid off and handed it to her. "Guess what I found?"

Elizabeth gasped. "The butterfly necklace!" She lifted it out. "How in the world...?"

He grinned. "You know how much I love estate auctions. The last time I was back in Palm Beach I went to one. Imagine my surprise. I found that and a few things that belonged to Merrell too. It was all at the same auction."

She hugged the pendant to her chest. "Thank you."

"Grandpa!" Sarah yelled. "Watch this." She did a cartwheel.

Hudson laughed. "Good job."

Sarah giggled as she spun across the playground.

Silence fell between them after that as they watched the kids play. Elizabeth continued gripping the necklace and her thoughts drifted back through the years...

"Everything okay?" He quietly asked a moment later. "I thought the necklace would make you happy."

"It does," she assured him. "Sorry. Sometimes I get caught up in memories. I'm a grown woman with a husband and a daughter, living a thousand miles from Palm Beach. I'm happy. A lot of years have gone by. Very few people knew the real Nora, you know?"

"Nora lived a dangerous life. Her end was inevitable."

Elizabeth glanced over at him. "Have you ever told anyone?"

"No, of course not. You?"

"No."

After Nora had drowned, Elizabeth just stood there in the storm staring at her mother floating in the water, surrounded by blood. She wasn't sure how long she stayed that way, but it was Hudson who walked through the sliding glass doors onto the terrace.

She was drunk and being mean.
She tripped and fell.
I could've saved her, but I didn't.

Those had been Elizabeth's words, delivered with no emotion. Hudson simply put his arm around her and led her back inside. After that, he handled everything.

The official story was that she tripped and fell, hit her head, and drowned.

Cooper and Raina knew the true details, but they didn't fault Elizabeth for not saving her mother.

Twenty years later and it remained a secret between the four of them.

Leaning over, he pressed a quick kiss to her cheek. "I've got a meeting. Tell our little daredevil I'll see her this weekend. By the way, I talked to Cooper this morning and he said to tell you hi."

"Hi back."

"You all still planning on coming to my place this weekend for a cookout?"

"Sounds good. Raina's visiting, so she'll be there too."

"Perfect."

Smiling, Elizabeth watched Hudson leave the park and climb into his black BMW. They exchanged one last wave and Elizabeth looked back across the park.

Sarah stood quietly behind a little boy with a jagged rock gripped in her fist as if she was about to stab him in the back.

Elizabeth shot to her feet. "Sarah!"

Slowly, her daughter turned just her head. She looked over her shoulder directly into her mother's eyes. Elizabeth's heart stopped when their gazes met.

Sneaky. Manipulative. Ugly.

Her daughter looked just like Nora.

ABOUT THE AUTHOR

S. E. Green is the award-winning, best-selling author of young adult and adult fiction. She grew up in Tennessee where she dreaded all things reading and writing. She didn't read her first book for enjoyment until she was twenty-five. After that, she was hooked! When she's not writing, she loves traveling and hanging out with a rogue armadillo that frequents her coastal Florida home.

BOOKS BY S. E. GREEN

Sister Sister

Ambition can be a bitch.

The Family

Be careful what you wish for…

The Lady Next Door

How well do you know your neighbor?

The Third Son

All he wants is a loving family to belong to…

Vanquished

A secret island. A sadistic society.

Monster

When the police need to crawl inside the mind of a monster, they call Caroline.

Killers Among

Everyone has a dark side.

Gone

One second. That's all it takes.